CW00854332

# The Light Of Friendship

D T Lewis-Dayle

D T Lewis-Dayle

"If you live to be a hundred, I hope to live to be a hundred minus one day, so that I never have to live a day without you" A A Milne.

D T Lewis-Dayle

# The Light Of Friendship

# D T Lewis-Dayle

Dedicated to:

Lee Scally;

Blue Eyes.

You truly are the definition of a best friend and a big brother with a massive heart. The one I trust implicitly and I wish you all the happiness that you truly deserve. Keep smiling, and here's to a lifetime of friendship.

"Thank you for always having my back"

I will forever appreciate the day that we met on the music video, Vampire by Lesbian Bed Death, 2021.

# The Light Of Friendship

# D T Lewis-Dayle

Acknowledgements.

Book Cover by Luke Saklatvala. Model Lee Scally.

Editor – Arlene McGlynn.


The author would like to also thank:

LHS Productions, Lesbian Bed Death, Naked Sunday, DE Caversmill and to those who believe.

# The Light Of Friendship

Chapter

Prologue

Epilogue.

D T Lewis-Dayle

# The Light Of Friendship

# D T Lewis-Dayle

## Prologue

From the shadows, the vampire watched the drunken woman stagger along the street alone. She was ripe for the picking and no one would miss her when she disappeared from life. He had already planned that immediately after taking the last swallow of her blood he would ditch her in one of the skips that littered the industrial estate. After all he had done that many times since turning into a night walker.

The sun was already rising and he felt weak as he kept as close to the walls to remain in shade as she circled the building seemingly singing some trashy boyband dance number. She vanished for a brief moment and as he peered into the grassy footpath that separated them, he noticed that she was actually urinating behind one of the large metallic bins.

He smiled to himself before realizing that he really should be disgusted, she didn't even use a sanitizer on her hands after she wiped down there with a tissue from her bra before tossing it to the ground. He considered ignoring this one and waiting for the next piece of breakfast that would walk on by but he was hungry and he hadn't seen food for some time and being a child of the night he had already been turned away from a number of bars and all you can eat buffets as he liked to call them; so really he had no choice.

She was getting closer, and as she waited he knew the element of surprise would work and by the time her screaming would stop he would be full and satisfied.

She was now here and he lurched into the air to frighten her as his face distorted to reveal his elongated fangs.

And that was when he realized that something was wrong. The green wetness streamed from his nostril and he had no choice but to flick the sticky nose goo with his finger to the ground.

"Cut" Cassidy called from behind the camera.

# The Light Of Friendship

People had started to laugh.

"Someone get him a tissue" Cassidy sighed, she was clearly annoyed that her morning was already wasted, "And I need a coffee"

"That never happened before" He smiled at the girl who responded with a shake of her head.

The vampire turned and smiled as the man dressed as a cop handed both him and the one called Cassidy a coffee.

"Cheers bud" The vampire took a sip out of the polystyrene cup after temporarily removed his decorative teeth.

"Places please" Cassidy called as she took her seat and she turned to the Vampire with a wry smile reflecting in her voice, "Can you try not to nose jizz on the cast please?"

The vampire tried not to laugh again through fear that the next thing ejecting from his nose would be the coffee that the policeman had just passed over.

"Screaming Queen's music video, Creature Of The Night Take Two" Cassidy called, with a cheeky glance over to the vampire, "And Lee... control your juices this time..."

# D T Lewis-Dayle

## 1 - The Love Of My Life.

My name is Lee Napier, and I am in my early thirties living in the small village of West Waterford with my girlfriend Margot. We had met three years earlier during one of my crazy nights out. Back in the day I was known as a wild one, and I would always have a shot glass or a pint in my hand and a hot woman on the other arm. My pals were always jealous that I would always take someone home but that one night changed me.

Margot Drake was on her own and I had just come back from the bathroom still buttoning up my ripped jeans and my jaw almost reached the floor as I drooled at her perfectly formed body that leant against the bar. I could see my friends Jack and Nathan on the dance floor dancing like maniacs trying to impress some girls that I had already made out with earlier and I chose to ignore them because I was taking that beautiful lady home.

She informed me that she had been abandoned by her mates and as I swooped in with a glass of wine by power of observation by the empty glass in her hand, and we went back to her place where we stayed up all night making love. She was different to anyone I had ever slept with and she made me feel complete. She loved me as I was, and her favourite past time would be to use her finger to trace the images of my tattoos, or she would twist my beard a little when she wanted to get frisky. Not that I needed the clues. We had cute little nicknames for each other, she liked to call me 'Scrumpy' because on my penchant for Cider, and I called her my 'Baby Doll' I loved her with all my heart.

# The Light Of Friendship

   We moved in above a florist a year later and I changed my life totally. Gone were the nights of uninhabited abandonment and in were nights of movies and our kitten Macy, a Siamese with a sarcastic attitude that could have easily matched mine. We named her Macy after her mother who had passed away soon after she was born, and although her father looked after her for a while, he drifted off into the sunset when she was just six, leaving her in a foster home.
   Life with Margot really made me the man I became. Before her, I would work nights in a dead-end warehouse job where I would monotonously label boxes of dog food, and then I would sleep, drink, slap myself about with whatever local talent would come my way, but she gave me the confidence to move on. I quit the job without thought and I got myself a job in a roleplaying agency, 'Wild Wolf World' where I would host parties as my favourite characters from the movies and I gradually made a few minor contacts.  My boss was a hot Goth chick named Cassidy but she was married to a complete moron in a very 'beauty and the beast' scenario.
   In time this led to a few small extra roles in television and I once even made an advertisement for a well-known breakfast cereal, and a voicing role for a cartoon series online. It was all down to my wonderful girlfriend.


   It was January 12th and the snow was heavy outside as I made my way into the office. Today was a special day, Margot was on her way home from being out of town with some of her family and she was about to turn 25 the very next day and I had planned a surprise party and I had chosen a ring that I was going to present to her at the right time.
   Cassidy was her usual miserable self as I approached my locker to store my leather jacket.

# D T Lewis-Dayle

"Bad news" She muttered, "It's a total whiteout, the roads over in Winchester are closed, and half of the guests will not be able to make it"

"As long the right people are there it doesn't matter" I smiled as I gently kissed my fingers and touched a small photograph I had of Margot that was glued into place on the door.

"Soppy bastard" She smiled.

"You're just jealous because you want a bit of me" I teased as I sauntered over to her desk, gesturing to the hairy man in the frame, I knew that his name was really Jesse, "Best you could get was a man that vaguely resembles a yeti with a bad haircut"

She giggled, "He will knock you out if he heard you speaking like that"

"I could take him" I posed flexing my muscles.

"Stop, you're making me moist" She sighed nonchalantly, "Anyway, I was speaking with a friend of mine about you. You did well on the music video. So much so that they want you to be their main star in the next couple of tracks"

"Great" I smiled.

"Promise me one thing Napier" She grinned as she took my hand, "Don't ever change"

"You mean that you want me to remain the sexy stud in the background that you can think about when you can't get off from your husband?" I questioned. She smiled back at me.

"So tonight's the night" She changed the subject, and I knew that she was dropping the hint that she wanted to see the ring again, so I withdrew it from my pocket.

# The Light Of Friendship

Margot greeted me with the longest most passionate kiss as she swung by the office upon her return. She was soaked with snow and she was shaking but I held enough heat in my body to warm her and she did not want to let go, even though the box that the ring was in pressed firm against her thigh.

"You pleased to see me Mr.?" She grinned.

I pulled her aside and before we knew it we were at it on Cassidy's desk, sending the framed photo of her hairy lover shattering to the floor as our clothes scattered across the room.

She wrapped her legs around me and pulled me in deeper and I stared into her eyes for long moments before kissing her perfect lips once more.

"I love you" I whispered with passion the moment I shot my seed joining her in orgasmic pleasure. I don't know whether it was because she had been gone for one night but I had missed her, it was barely a few pumps and a squirt.

We kissed more as we dressed, and as she finally located her panties on one of the plants, she scrunched them up and placed them in my pocket, "Something to remind you of me whilst I go home and freshen up"

She turned to walk away but I took her hand to pull her back for one more kiss.

She pulled away, "I have to go"

"What's wrong?" I questioned.

"You've had your wicked way Scrumpy" She grinned as she placed her finger on my lips, "If I don't get home now, I will be late for my own party"

Something was wrong and the fear inside me began to eat at me.

She walked out of the room, and as she paused at the doorway, she smiled, "Trust me, tonight is going to be perfect"

## D T Lewis-Dayle

I hated myself for allowing my mind to wander. In the three years we were together we had never spent more than a night away but she seemed different now. I felt nervous as I approached the venue called "Woodies" that I had hired for the party. It was by reputation a little back street slum bar but the regulars had called it home. I could see from the outside that some people were already there and from the sound that emerged from inside that the party had already started, but as I pushed open the door, the room silenced.

"You should have been keeping watch for him" Someone hissed, and I knew straight away it was one of my friends. The light instantly switched off, "Bit late know dickhead"

"What is going on?" I commanded.

A spotlight fell onto the floor, and I was graced by the beauty that was Margot encased in a blue hue that emphasized everything that I loved about her. She stood silently for a moment as my favourite rock ballad commenced and she slowly raised the microphone.

"Lee Napier" She smiled when I expected her to sing, she lowered herself to her knee and produced a silver ring from her pocket, "I have loved you for the last three years, so I think it's time that you make an honest woman out of me…"

"Yes" I accepted and I too took out the ring that I had chosen, and we placed them lovingly onto each-others fingers, "I will never let you go… ever"

## 2 - The End.

We kissed for what seemed like an eternity, amidst a rapturous applause from our guests, although I think some of them may have started to get bored of the Margot and Lee snog fest because by the time the lights returned, people were already at the bar.

"I knew what you were up to" Margot confessed as we embraced, "You were as subtle as a brick"

"I thought that I was being romantic" I snuggled up to her, "When did you find out?"

"Months ago when you left the receipt for this gorgeous ring in your jeans" She kissed me again, "I did a laundry load and I had to turn out your pockets"

I blushed and I kissed her again, as I felt someone tap my shoulder.

"You owe me a new photo-frame" Cassidy smiled, "And if I ever find out that you had sex on my desk again I will rip it off"

The colour once more rushed to my cheeks, not only because my boss's comments but my fiancé's hands were gripping wantonly at my butt.

Eventually we stopped kissing long enough for our guests to celebrate our engagement and the party really started. Instead of the traditional soft loving music people could smooch to, we favoured rock music and gin, and although the room was filled with our friends, it would not have mattered to me if we were alone.

# D T Lewis-Dayle

"I have to admit" A familiar voice spoke, distracting me from the beauty before me, I turned and smiled at one of my oldest acquaintances Jack who had left West Waterford almost two years ago when he took a job in Australia, we instantly embraced before he could even finish his sentence, "I never thought that I would meet the woman that could tame you"

"The past is in the past" I confessed as I lovingly glanced over to her chatting away animatedly to some of the girls that she worked with, "She's the one"

"You two are great together" He agreed.

"What about you?" I queried, "How is life Down Under?"

"Perfect" He nodded, distracted by someone at the bar, "Listen, I will catch up with you shortly"

He brushed past me and disappeared into the crowd, but I was not alone for long when Cassidy cornered me once more, with a gift and a grin, "You deserve everything that is coming your way"

I smiled as I tore open the envelope that she had passed me, I read the message aloud, "Congratulations on becoming partner in Wild Wolf World"

"You're the finest act that I have on the books. Nobody brings in as much work as you do and only last week you yourself you had someone recognize you whilst waiting for a train to the film set. This is the kind of promotion we need" She explained.

I recalled that moment the young mother approached me to ask me for an autograph for her son who recognized me from voicing one of his favourite cartoon characters. It amazed me to realise that I was now being noticed for my work. Once more another thing that I could thank Margot for, if it wasn't for her, I would still be in the warehouse and I was grateful for everything that she did for me.

# The Light Of Friendship

We were distracted for a moment when her husband Jesse returned from the bar with a drink and pulled her away from me.

I don't recall seeing Jack after he wandered into the crowds, but as midnight approached and the guests dispersed, only a handful of people stayed for the last orders.

"Have you thought of dates?" She queried as she sipped on a glass of wine.

"All I want to do is to spend the rest of our lives together" I confessed. I had planned everything pretty much down to the finest detail.

The wedding was going to take place in a vineyard that we once visited at Halloween, and I had already booked the honeymoon to Brazil, somewhere that I knew that she had always wanted to visit and now that I had become partner I wasn't going to be short on cash any time soon.

"Something that I always remember one of my best friends saying to me was 'why settle for silver when I can have gold?'" She leaned in for a kiss, "I am glad that I found my gold"

"I am so lucky that I have found you" I agreed.

By 01.30 Margot had vanished into the ladies with some of the ladies, and I recognized a lone figure at the bar. He definitely was not here throughout the evening because I had personally spoken to everyone. As I approached him, he seemed lost and alone.

"This is a private party" I began to explain.

He turned and I smiled. It was the guy who was the cop on the music video a few days ago, the one who delivered me a coffee after I released the nose dribble on that poor unfortunate young lady.

"I'm sorry" I extended my hand, "I'm useless with names"

"Chris Scott" He responded with a grin that seemed infectious, "Sorry to gatecrash, but Cassidy told me about the party. I would have gotten here earlier but I was out of town and the weather was abysmal"

"It's good that you came" I don't know why I said that because I had never met the bloke before, "The more people that see me happy, the merrier"

"You deserve it mate" He grinned as he embraced me for a hug. This took me aback as I was not an affectionate person, but for some reason, it felt right, "Margot is a wonderful woman and she makes you happy. Therefore she is perfect for you"

I found myself warming toward him, and I briefly told him everything that I could about her. I hadn't had a real friend for some time. I think that the last one was Tommy Basford who turned out to be a complete bastard and the last that I heard was that he was doing time for ABH.

Minutes later he input his digits on my phone, "If you ever need me, you can call me day or night"

"Thank you" I felt sincere because although I had associates, something about Chris seemed different, "She turned my life around"

"It is what we all look for in life" He turned away as he finished his beer, "I guess I will see you around"

He didn't give me any chance to respond as he walked away with some of the guests that were leaving.

I turned on my heels and sighed as I noticed the last of our friends had also left.

"Do you want to go out to a nightclub?" My fiancé smiled as she sauntered toward me.

"No" I kissed her again, "I want to start our life together horizontally"

# The Light Of Friendship

I reached over to her shoulder and removed a single white feather that had perched on her dress, and I flicked it to the ground.

She grabbed my hand and guided me out into the brisk cold air.

We lived just minutes away from the bar so there was no need for a cab. We held hands and the seconds seemed like hours but I was with the woman that I loved and it was all that I needed. We didn't even care that the snow was falling heavily again.

"Napier" A voice called from the shadows.

In synchronicity we both turned to face the hefty silhouette emerge from behind several parked cars that were either abandoned by revelers that had attended our party and were probably staying nearby.

"You owe me" The shadowy figure snarled.

My eyes drew down to his side and I noticed the silver glint of a blade before he emerged into the moonlight.

"Jack what the..." I began.

I stopped as I sensed his anger by the way that he marched forcefully towards us, instinctively I blocked Margot from him.

"Why do you get the perfect life? The managerial position and the pay rise?" He questioned, "When we know all about your past"

I became aware that other people were nearby, someone stood to my immediate left, and another slightly behind us.

"Whatever this is about we can talk about this" I tried to calm him.

# D T Lewis-Dayle

The knife rose and on impulse I slipped back into Kung-Fu mode whilst protecting my future wife. I felt a sting in one of my thighs as my legs became windmills and I kicked the blade out of Jack's hand and I knew instantly that I had hurt him as he fell to the floor for a moment. He must have forgotten that I was a Black belt in the martial art.

The other two assailants ran off somewhere during the madness.

"You won't get away with this" Jack snarled, "She will know the truth"

"I don't know what you are on about" I retaliated.

"You think that you're the omnipotent Lee Napier, but I am going to bring you down to the bowels of hell where you belong" He was standing upright now.

"What the hell happened to you in Australia?" I questioned as I lunged forward, he reacted by turning and running back into the shadows.

I waited for a moment to confirm that he had gone before I turned back. I could see dark patches of blood in the snow and then I saw her motionless on the ground.

I screamed her name as I rushed to her side but my 'Baby Doll' was already gone.

# The Light Of Friendship

### 3 - Chris.

Her funeral was held on a Wednesday. I walked behind the horse drawn carriage with a single black rose in my hand. She was certified dead that same night by the paramedics that tried their best to treat her. My heart was well and truly broken. She was buried in a grave next to her mother and some harpist played some cheesy soft halo music that I knew she would have despised. I recall spotting Chris with a curly haired blonde woman in the crowd both in the church and at the wake but I chose not to talk to him, I favoured my own space, and cider.

I locked myself away from the world and it was just Macy the cat and I for now. She knew that her mummy was gone and it took her a while to adjust to life without Margot and our home became both a shrine to my fiancé and a mess because I could not be bothered to clean and I lived on take out. I hated the fact that throughout the whole incident I only sustained a tiny little scratch on my thigh whilst my lovely wife-to-be was dead.

The blackness of loneliness took over and I tried to sleep as much as I could just so that I could still be with her my dreams. I longed for those lucid ones that meant that I could touch her body and smell her as though she was still here and I would wake either holding the pillow, or my legs were wrapped tight around it that it was misshapen. My days became shorter as I chose to drink whisky to numb the pain and it helped me to drift off to slumber.

# D T Lewis-Dayle

"You won't get away with this" Jack's words often echoed through my mind often. I did not know what he had meant. I accept that I was not the most angelic of people and that I had a past as a ladies man but I had never even got a parking ticket. Margot knew everything about me and we had no secrets.

Jack evaded capture by taking his own life in his flat and it soon transpired that he had been fired from his job several months ago and was up to his eyeballs in debt. Two other men were arrested and charged with the murder but I could not face them in court.

It took me a few months to gather the energy to return to work, and Cassidy welcomed me back with open arms and a caring shoulder to cry on. It was at that moment when I took her over the same desk, I remembered her telling me that I owed her a new photo-frame. We started to have sex at any given opportunity but the first time I slept with her in the same bed that she shared with her yeti-like husband, I felt guilty. I cried in the shower the next day because I had betrayed my one true love. I consoled myself that I thought of Margot all along, which I continued as Cassidy and I embarked on an affair, but despite this, I hated myself when I went home alone. It wasn't long before Macy picked up the scent and she left soon after. Perhaps I deserved to be alone now.

It was a Friday evening almost three months since the funeral when I plucked up the courage to venture out to Woodies again. It was exactly the same as before. The same buxom barmaid served the same people and the bearded biker owner entertained the masses with his acoustic rock ballads. The room silenced for a moment as I entered.

# The Light Of Friendship

"As you were" I sighed. I was tired of the sympathetic head tilts and shoulder touches that people gave. I ordered a pint and I took a table near to the window briefly. I moved as I spotted the road in which Margot had died, and I opted to move closer to the pool table.

Two inept players were hitting and hoping and I smiled to myself as the white ball shot across the floor for a moment. As the girl retrieved it, I noticed the smiling man with the cue in his hand.

"Sorry about that" He apologized, "I was never good at aiming"

"Hello Chris" I greeted him like an old friend with a warm embrace as I joined them.

"This is my partner Taryn" He introduced the blushing blonde, "We were just passing though, I was going to call you tomorrow to see if you wanted to catch up"

"I would have liked that" I confessed, I must admit that it felt good to speak with someone who I knew would not judge me, yet I barely knew anything about him.

"I think I will leave you two to it" Taryn smiled with a beautiful Irish accent, as she greeted Chris with a gentle kiss on the lips.

"You don't have to leave on my account" I felt terrible that she didn't want to be here.

"I need to make a call to my boss" She grinned as she passed me the white ball, "Beside I am useless at this game, I think that Chris needs a challenge"

I glanced over and Chris was already setting up a new game.

"Don't be long" She turned to her boyfriend, "We have to be on the way first thing"

She kissed him again and walked toward the door.

"She's beautiful mate" I admit that I watched her a little too long as she walked.

# D T Lewis-Dayle

"She's something" He agreed, "We only just got together recently. We met on a film set, she was a nun and I was a rabid rabbit"

"That makes no sense" I laughed.

"It was a horror film" He confessed, "Straight to DVD, but it was worth it"

"Perhaps you can refer me to one of your director friends?" I pressed, it was always wise to network.

"Actually" He began to chalk the cue, "There may be an opportunity coming up for the role of a vampire in a semi-large budget movie being filmed in Scotland... If you're interested?"

"Am I ever?" I exclaimed.

"Then, keep your diary free my friend" He used the touch of the shoulder technique, "Our friendship is going to be a fun one filled with film cameras..."

He surprised me at his pool skills as he won four games straight although I think he allowed me to win the fifth game. He must have been faking his uselessness at the game with his partner. I was usually the king of this game but this man taught me a lesson or two. He took one trick shot after another and left seven of my balls on the table on more than one occasion.

# The Light Of Friendship

We shook hands and we bought each other rounds of beer. I felt like I had known Chris for life. I knew that at twenty-seven he was the youngest of four children, he had lived all over the world for his job and that he was a part-time professional singer on the cruise liners before he settled down in Middleton as a freelance talent scout. He had never had children but hoped that Taryn and he could try once they were married. I found myself talking more about myself and I could tell that this man was listening to me. He knew that my heart was irreparable at the moment, but when he touched my shoulder, and whispered, 'You will be happy again one day' I began to cry.

He whispered something almost inaudible to me as he embraced me.

"What did you just say?" I asked.

"You're a star" He repeated, "Whatever happens, you will always have me as friend"

"Star" I smiled, the word felt right.

It was almost midnight as we left Woodies. I could hear the sound of sirens in the distance and for a brief moment it bought back the moment that Margot died in my arms but Chris had a sense of calm about him.

"When are you next in town?" I queried.

"Soon" He responded, "Perhaps we can have a rematch"

"Deal" I smiled, as he stopped to reply to a message on his mobile. I waited for him out of courtesy before continuing, "There's an all-night diner a short walk from here if you are up for something to eat?"

"That's ok, I am not hungry" He responded, and then he raised his head, "Tell me something Lee, are you settling alright since the incident? I know that grieving can take some time so I just want to check in on you from time to time"

# D T Lewis-Dayle

For the first time I realized that he had actually enquired direct.

I nodded, "I have never had a friend that I could actually talk to about things"

"I promise that I will always be here as a shoulder to cry on, or if you want to pick up the phone I will be there as soon as I can"

He turned and commenced walking away.

"Chris" I called, "Will you be back soon?"

He did not answer.

The Light Of Friendship

## 4 – The Lady In Denim.

The following morning, I switched on the television as I made a coffee, and I sighed as news reports showed that a fatal car accident had happened just outside of town last night killing the sole driver, a teenager called Jay. That must have been the sirens that I had heard yesterday. I switched over to a cartoon just as the parents were shown grieving. I had suffered enough pain myself, I could not watch another. A sharp pain shot through my left thigh where I had been stabbed, and I gently stroked it to soothe the discomfort.

Cassidy was not in the office when I arrived, and she turned up whilst I was making a coffee. She sat away from me and switched on the PC. Without words I placed her mug next to her.

"Polly Anna from The Screaming Queens wants to meet you for lunch" She muttered without turning to me, "She has the contract, I need you to sign it and bring it in tomorrow so I can send to the solicitor"

She gestured to a post-it note that lay at an uncomfortable angle that I knew she did not want to face me.

"What's happened?" I questioned.

"Jesse knows" She sighed, "Everything"

I felt like an idiot for my next question, "About?"

She placed the photographic frame face down on the desk, "He knows that we have had sex here and in our marital bed. He hates me"

I wanted to place a caring hand on her shoulder as I sensed that she was crying.

# D T Lewis-Dayle

"He threw me out last night" She continued, "I am staying with my sister until I get something sorted, but I don't want you to be around here. Can you work from home and communicate only through email?"

"Sure" I agreed.

"I understand that you are grieving but you can't just fall into the vagina to make you feel better" She was still talking and whilst I found the phrase amusing I refrained from giggling, "I want you to leave now. I will come in late tomorrow to co-sign the contract. I don't want to see you"

I nodded. I don't even know why I reacted this way she wasn't even paying attention to me.

Silently I retrieved the note and returned to my locker. As I tore open the door I smiled at the photograph of Margot and touched her face. I put on my leather jacket and checked that the mobile and cash card was in the pocket. I tried once more to see her face as I left but she was already on to me and she turned away.

Her ghosting hurt me. I felt betrayed by my friend and my heart was splitting in two again. Yes I knew that I should not have slept with her not only for Margot but also because she was married. I was never this man. I began to shake as I walked toward the restaurant called 'Rumana' that Polly Anna had chosen to meet. I sank a few glasses of whisky at one of the cheap bars nearby because I knew that this restaurant charged a small fortune. Thankfully, I knew that this was on Polly Anna and The Screaming Queens but I had to play safe. I wanted to text Cassidy to check in on her but I had to accept that she made the request for me to only contact for work and through email.

"Nice one Lee" I sighed to myself, "You wrecked one of your only friendships you have left"

# The Light Of Friendship

That wasn't true. I knew deep within my own heart that she was not truly abandoning me after all she had just given me shares in the company, and I also had Chris, wherever he was.

Polly Anna was the black and red haired lead singer of the band and I have to admit that I felt attracted to her from the moment I had met her. She was a typical goth girl dressed in black and purple, with piercings and crazy make-up that made her stand out from the modern woman.

She extended a fingerless gloved hand with decorated nails, and shook with a firm grip, "It's good to see you again Lee"

"Thank you" I greeted as I allowed her to sit before me.

"Let's get straight down to business" She smiled with an eager grin and added almost my own thoughts, "This place charges the air that you breath so I don't want to be here much longer than it takes for a ham sandwich and a couple of shots"

She pushed over the envelope which I opened and studied briefly as the waitress approached for our order. Once we surveyed the extortionate menu I opted for one of the tiniest chicken wings I had ever seen and a pint of cider before returning my gaze to the contract. I could sense that she was watching me with those big blue eyes, and then I felt her hand touch my thigh.

"When I first watched the Creature of The Night music video, I thought to myself 'Now there's a piece of meat I wouldn't mind chewing on" She purred, tightening her grip, "I was so sorry to hear that your wife was murdered"

"We weren't married" I spoke, trying to remove her hand from my anatomy.

"I have never seen a dead body before" She was an ignorant hot mess, and I just wanted to get this paperwork done. She continued, "What say we blow this joint and go back to yours for a quick game of hide the sausage?"

## D T Lewis-Dayle

I raised my head to speak, but something caught my eye near to the bar. I rose and slowly made my way through the crowd. The blonde woman moved from my view for a moment and I panicked. Surely it could not be. I scanned the room and noted the ladies bathroom door swing, and I saw her again, just a wisp of blonde swept over her denim jacket.

"I heard rumour that you were keen" Polly Anna continued to chatter by my side.

I turned to face her, "I will sign the contract"

"I paid the bill, so I am ready when you are stud" She stroked my arm. I wanted so much to slap this annoying sexy woman.

"I just need to talk to someone" I interrupted before she could say anything more, "I will be right down once I speak to my friend"

"Red Toyota outside" She smiled, as she cupped my buttocks and leaned in for a kiss.

I pushed her away gently, "Save it for the bedroom"

I waited for fifteen minutes like a creepy man outside the ladies bathroom. I could sense that some of the customers were questioning what I was doing. I was certain that I had seen her but she never emerged from the cubicles.

As I stepped outside, Polly Anna was waiting impatiently in her magnificent mode of transport. My mind flashed back to what Cassidy had said to me earlier about sleeping around. I simply shook my head and commenced walking the opposite way of what I needed. Moments later she tore past me and I was almost certain that she flipped me the bird.

# The Light Of Friendship

      I walked for what felt like an hour, but in reality I was only a mile away from where I started. It was eerily familiar and as I stopped outside the metallic gate I recoiled in horror as I recalled that the last time that I was here, I buried my fiancé.  In the distance I could see a congregation, and I allowed my eyes to move slowly along the headstones, and then I saw the denim wearing blonde again.

My feet started to move and I stepped closer toward the woman.

She remained stationary on the steps of the church, clutching a book of sorts. My heart was racing as I gathered pace. The congregation had shifted and were making their way towards me, and as they merged in front of the same stairs, the blonde woman had either entered, or vanished along with the people.

I wanted to call her name as I frantically searched the crowd again, but I did not know anybody with me and they had just been standing at the grave of a beloved one.

"Sir" A voice disrupted me. I turned and smiled at the priest that was tending to a nearby grave. "You look a little spooked"

"My girlfriend" I muttered, "I have just seen my Margot"

The priest nodded.

"She died" I felt myself cry.

# D T Lewis-Dayle

## 5 – The Priest & The Scorned Lover.

The priest made me a sweet tea which I caressed as I took to one of the pews. I always had the belief that I would burst into flames if I ever entered a house of God, so it surprised me that I was inside the same place where I had buried Margot Drake just a few months ago. I had not been back to the site since because I could not bring myself to go back.

"I remember that day" The priest spoke in a monotone, yet caring voice, "You could not speak and would not let anyone comfort you. You walked at least six feet in front of everyone and insisted that you stood alone as we lowered the coffin"

I raised my tear stained face as he sipped on his cup to pause for a moment, "I miss her"

"Grief is one of those situations that we all must take at some point and there is never a time limit to it. One man may grieve for as little as a year, whereas another may take a lifetime to get over their loss. There is no right or wrong answer. I recall a particular lady at my first parish. Her name was Mary and she was in her thirties when her first husband passed away. I cannot remember his name but about two years later she came to see me and she was getting married again. She had many doubts and in the end I married her to her second husband. They spent another twenty years together deeply in love, and when he died she told me that she still mourned her first husband every day" He explained, "I guess what I am saying is you are free to move on when the time is right for you, and I am sure that Margot would condone it"

.

# The Light Of Friendship

"I don't want to" I was shaking. I could not recall what I had said in the moments between being outside and him making me a tea. I must have mentioned what had happened with either Cassidy or Polly Anna.

The priest simply smiled, "When you are ready, you will know it"

"Could it be possible that I have just seen her ghost?" I questioned.

"It is quite possible that she is using a veil to pass you a message from the other side to give you peace of mind" He agreed, "The Lord will work in mysterious ways"

"I've never been a church goer" I confessed, "Why would I be so special?"

"You should never chastise yourself for wanting to see the lady that you loved in the afterlife" He continued, and then paused again, "Do you think that it's time that you paid her a visit?"

I shook my head, "I can't"

"Listen to me" He advised, "Someone out there is going to be very special to you during mourning. It may be something that they may say or do, but they will help you however possible. It could be somebody that you knew many years ago or it might be one that you have not even met yet…"

"I have met a new person recently" I nodded as I thought of my new friend Chris.

"Tell me about this person" He pressed.

"I met him on a music video set earlier in the year and then he turned up at the engagement party" I found myself smiling, "We hit it off straight away, we just became friends and I don't have many of them. The last one killed Margot"

I noted that the priest was nodding along as he listened to me.

"I guess I never had someone like him before which is why I value him" I continued, and I felt my head bob in agreement, "I will talk to him and I promise I will listen. I think that he is the one that will help me through this"

I withdrew my mobile telephone and searched the gallery for some photographs. I soon located one of us both during one of our pool games.

"Is that him?" He questioned.

"He really has become someone that I can rely on" I noticed that the priest seemed taken aback by the person in the picture, "Is everything alright?"

"He looks…." The priest began and then smiled as he passed me back my property, "He looks like a nice boy"

"He is" I found myself agreeing, "I don't think I would have coped if it wasn't for him coming into my life when he did…"

I sat on a bench at a nearby lakeside, watching the lovers on their picnic dates or the dog-walkers enjoying themselves. I thought back to the priest telling me that 'when I was ready I would know' and I wandered to myself if it was really something that I wanted to do. I blew onto the polystyrene cup of coffee that I had purchased and thought about her. Perhaps that is why I saw the woman in denim and made a presumption that it was Margot.

I tried to remember the face of the ghost but I was not certain that it was Margot now. Maybe I had projected the image onto an innocent person that I had seen twice.

"There is no such thing as ghosts" I confessed to myself.

# The Light Of Friendship

I chose to try a different bar that evening, a rockers bar called Roxy's over in the neighbouring district of East Waterford. I had not been there since I had met Margot. It was not as I remembered it. Where the juke box used to be was a bandana-wearing DJ, where the mosh pit was now stood a new bar that was decorated with rails all around to protect the staff and the music seemed to be a more gentle style of rock that what I recall. I must have been getting old because I did not recognize anybody.

I took the words from the priest with me, and as I glanced across the room again, I wanted to see Margot again. I knew that there was no way I would see her again but my mind wanted to create everyone in her image.

The last time we were in here together was a week before the incident. We had been caught making love in the toilets by security, who simply just watched us rather than tear us apart. The freak. I watched a particularly young looking girl grinding against one of the poles and I shook the vision of Margot away.

That was not how I wanted to remember her.

After a couple of draught beers I decided that Roxy's was no longer the place that it used to be and I found myself looking at my watch longing for the next bus back to West Waterford. I still had almost an hour and there was no other location in this dead end town so I ordered yet another over-foamed lager from the miserable barmaid and sat in the window watching the world go by.

People outside seemed to be enjoying themselves and I wanted to be like them. Happy again.

I was soon distracted by a large reflection in the window that spoke before I could even turn, "What the hell are you doing here?"

# D T Lewis-Dayle

"Alright Jesse" I rose still facing away from him.

"Turn when you talk to me you maggot" He insisted.

I knew from the redness in the small space of cheek that showed from his overly hairy face that he was angry.

"You dare to walk into my establishment after what you did" He commanded an answer and I could sense that the rest of the customers had stopped their evening activity to see what was happening.

I casually took a sip of my drink and placed it carefully on the table before me, "I was grieving"

"With my wife" He spat.

I started to turn to him but then I saw the woman again outside. She was talking to someone that was just outside my line of sight. I wanted to tap on the glass to gain her attention but then I realised that Jesse was about to challenge me. But then I didn't want to lose her again.

"I didn't mean to do it" I found myself confessing.

I then felt his rough hand against my neck and as I searched for my Margot again I felt the glass window shatter under the weight of my body and I landed in a heap on the patio outside. I rose almost instantly and ignored the scratches of blood. I could tell by the laughter that this man was accompanied by admiring females. Cassidy deserved better than that Neanderthal.

"You stay away from my pub and my wife" Jesse snarled from the broken frame, "If I ever catch you even looking sideways at Cassidy again I swear you will be reunited with your lover in record time"

Although I wanted to teach him a lesson for bashing me, I opted to turn and walk away amidst an array of abuse from the scorned husband. He was right though. I knew that I should never have slept with her and once more I hated myself for what I had done to another human.

# The Light Of Friendship

I felt my hand reach for my mobile and as I walked I searched my contacts and stopped at the name Chris, and I pressed dial.

"I need a friend" I admitted.

"I'm on my way" He responded.

Chris spoke with me all the time. I knew that he did not want to close the call without knowing that I was ok. Every time that I wanted to stop he would listen to me and advise me that he was on his way. I felt comforted because I had never had a buddy that would actually drop whatever they were doing to be there for me. What did I do to deserve this remarkable human to come into my life just at the right time?

By the time he arrived, I collapsed in his arms in the middle of the night. I allowed the tears to flow freely as the events of the day got on top of me.

"I really need a pal now" I broke down and allowed him to guide me to one of the benches nearby.

# D T Lewis-Dayle

## 6 – Why Settle For Silver?

I don't know how long I wept for. He placed his caring hand on my shoulder as I flooded the top of his head with the salt water tears that I could no longer control. Somehow he guided me to a bench and through my own blurred vision I noticed that we were back in the cemetery where the love of my life was buried.

It took me a while to gather my thoughts and although Chris did not speak or pressure me to talk, I felt safe as he stroked my hair. The last time someone did that was Margot; I think maybe I must have been a puppy in my previous life.

Eventually, after what seemed like hours, I spoke, "Thank you. I haven't got anybody that would drop whatever they are doing just to come to me when I needed"

"I will always be there" He responded, "And if all you want to do is sit in silence, then I will do so too. No pressure"

I nodded, as I gathered my thoughts in order so I could explain to him why I needed a friend. It seemed like another hour passed whilst I did so.

"Do you believe in ghosts?" I asked.

"Of course I do" His response was instant.

"I saw her" I sighed, "Margot"

He did not respond, and I knew that he wanted me to continue.

"I haven't been able to bring myself to visit her since the funeral but I have seen her a few times. The first time was in a restaurant and I saw her go into the bathroom. I waited for a while but she never came back. Then I found myself here in the grave yard and I saw her at a graveside but she disappeared into a crowd" I explained, "The priest spoke with me and asked me if I wanted to visit her but I cannot"

# The Light Of Friendship

"It seems strange that she vanished without talking to you" He spoke, "Usually when an apparition appears they want to pass you a message"

I pulled away from him and looked into his eyes, "Why would she not want to talk to me?"

"Perhaps she is not ready, like you?" He offered with a gentle shrug.

"I just want her back so much" I felt the tears flowing again and my words were coming out in a stammer which I had not done for years. I hated that I felt so weak, and I collapsed once more into his welcoming arm.

I cried again for some time and even though I felt silly for it Chris made me calm. I asked myself if this is what a friend really was. He asked me two separate times if I was fine, and I responded with a single nod.

"I have a gift for you" He smiled when I lit a cigarette, uncertain of how long we had been sitting in the middle of cemetery during the early hours.

"You don't have to get me anything, friendship is all I want" I inhaled on the smoke.

"I know I don't have to" He responded as he opened his satchel, "I wanted to, and it is my job to make you smile"

He presented me a scroll wrapped with a wax sealed ribbon. I read the label, 'To the best human in the world Lee, this is because you are one'

"What's this?" I questioned, breaking the seal.

It unrolled in my hand and I read aloud, "You really are a star my friend, and the world is at your feet"

"I believe in you" He grinned.

"Why would you do this?" My voice cracked and I knew that I was going to cry. I stopped myself and leaned in to hug him one more time.

# D T Lewis-Dayle

"Because once in a while, someone special comes along and makes you realise that it's ok to break down and cry, we are all human" He explained, "So I wanted to give you the deed to a star so that whenever you feel like you have nothing or nobody, you can look up and know that someone really does care about you"

"That's beautiful mate" I tried to hold back the tears, I had only known this man for a short while and I have done nothing but cry to him.

He searched the skies and then pointed to the constellation of Cassiopeia, the queen "It's that one Lee. I dated it June 1st for you as a Gemini"

"My birthday" I gasped.

I knew quite a bit about the stars, and as I glanced at the 'W' formation, I took one look at my friend and I realised that he was a true friend. I placed my hand onto his shoulder and finally allowed a tear to fall.


This time I sat next to him deep in thought. This person came into my life on a music video just months ago and he knew more about me than anyone I had known for years. My mind ran through what I knew about him.

"Chris" I broke the silence, "It's a pleasure to call you my best friend but I see you more as a brother"

"I like that" He responded.

"You really came through for me when I needed it so I would like to return the favour" I continued, as I rose and invited him to hug me once more, "I think I would like to visit the grave"

"Are you certain?" He questioned.

I nodded.

"I don't think that it is the right time" He retorted.

"Yes" I agreed, "Not in the middle of the night"

# The Light Of Friendship

He nodded, "Let's get you home and if you want me to come with you to see Margot, let me know and I will be there"

"You're always going to be there for me" I knew that he was genuine and I wanted to allow yet another tear fall onto my beard, and with Chris it really did not matter, "I think it's time I went home to get some sleep"

I started to walk, and he stopped me and guided me to another exit, "This way is quickest"

I listened to him and together we stepped along the graveled pathway.

We arrived outside my home just before 03:30 and for a brief moment I thought that I saw Macy in the window and my heart sank as I recalled that she had left me as it dawned on me that it was a simple shadow.

"Thank you for tonight" I shook his hand.

"Make sure you put some salt water on those wounds" He gestured toward my scratches, and I nodded.

"It's late so you can sleep on the couch if you want?" I offered.

"No it is alright" He seemed standoffish, "I need to get back for Taryn"

"Ok" I kind of felt hurt that he was keen to leave. I removed my keys from my pocket and turned back to my flat.

"I hit the jackpot when I met her" He commented, "Like she always said, 'Why settle for silver when you can have gold...'"

I didn't hear what he continued to say because that statement lingered in the air. His jovial persona angered me because Margot used to say that to me, and I felt the red mist raise within me.

"Why did you just say that?" I seethed.

# D T Lewis-Dayle

I span on one foot, and raised the other high creating a single blade windmill again, and I knew instantly that I had hurt him as he fell to the left as my lower limb met his face. He cried in pain the most gut-wrenching scream that I had heard, and he dropped to the ground in an instant.

Fear took over the anger and I stopped. What had I done to him?

"Chris I am sorry" Although I begged I did not move, I think that I was frozen in fear on the spot.

He did not move, "Stay away from me"

I wanted to help him back to his feet but something was stopping me.

My best friend was a weakened heap of a shivering pathetic mess that I had caused and he was too scared to move before me. I didn't blame him because when I used to compete in regional competitions I always won but I had no reason to do this to him.

"Please" My lip started to quiver, "I didn't mean to hurt you"

"I will forgive you" I heard him cry from his hidden state, "But for now I want you to leave me alone"

"I cannot abandon you" I pleaded.

"Just go" He commanded, still hidden.

I nodded and turned my back to him, "Please forgive me"

Those ten steps to my own front door had never seemed so far, and I hated myself more than ever before. As I inserted the key, I dared to turn back to him. But he was gone. He must have fled me when he had the chance.

"I'm so sorry" I cried.

My head was spinning as I entered my bathroom, I caught my own reflection in my mirror and I despised the man before me.

# The Light Of Friendship

"You don't deserve to be happy" I yelled, punching the reflective glass creating a satisfying cobweb of fine lines under the force of the fist.

I watched as several shards splintered off into the sink and instinct told me to pick up the biggest piece. I gritted my teeth and pressed it against my wrist and I was relieved as I saw the redness of my blood started to spill and I stopped.

D T Lewis-Dayle

### 7 – Wild Wolf World.

I could hear the gentle vibration of my phone in my jeans. I contemplated not answering it but whomever it was, well they were being impatient. No sooner did it go through to my automated voicemail they rang again. I carefully placed the blade next to the taps and I withdrew my mobile. Chris was calling me.

"What?" I spat.

"Look outside" He commented.

I took a deep breath, he really was the last person that I wanted to see right now. My bathroom was in the back of the house so I made my way through to the lounge and pushed back the curtain.

He raised a hand, still on the phone, "Come down to me"

I tossed the phone onto the couch and I made my way back down the staircase. I did not want to see him, but those last few minutes seemed like hours. I paused for a minute at the door before opening it.

He stood alone underneath the street light.

"What do you want?" I asked.

"Lee Napier, I forgive you for assaulting me" He spoke, and as he did, I noticed that his nose was covered in blood and my heart sank as I realised that I had done him physical damage. He continued, "I got about fifty steps away before I wanted to let you know that I am the type of guy who will be willing to let you hit me if you needed it because you need to release some stress. Because I will rather you hurt me than yourself or anyone else"

"I would never do that in normal circumstances" I responded.

# The Light Of Friendship

"Yet you didn't retaliate to Jesse when he pushed you through the window" He retaliated, "Brother that means you are a stronger man than you believe"

I moved toward him and put out his hands to stop me.

"Whilst I forgive you for drop-kicking me, I need you stay away until I call you again" He seemed like he was scared of me. I nodded to allow him to know that I understood. "You scared me earlier"

"Sorry" I mouthed, unsure if the words actually left my lips.

"You really do deserve to be happy Lee" He finalised as he turned away, "I promise no matter what happens, as your friend I will make you smile, somehow"

That was the longest week of my life whilst I waited for him to message me. He seemed to disappear off the face of the earth but then one lunch time I received a text message from him just simply stating he would meet me for a coffee the next day. I had a weird spring in my step just by receiving that, and within seconds, I received a call from Cassidy asking me to come into the office. I sprayed my nicest cologne because I have to admit I hadn't really paid much attention to my personal hygiene recently. If it smelt clean I considered it was so the aftershave would disguise anything disgusting about me.

It surprised me that she seemed chirpier than last time I had seen her. She had a smile on her face and she presented me with two enveloped as I perched on her desk.

"The first one is the contract from The Screaming Queens video" She tapped on the top one, "You need to be in Palma on Monday for the next video, the details are in the contract"

"You're looking well" I smiled. It had been a week and her entire personality had changed.

# D T Lewis-Dayle

"Jesse has filed for a divorce because of my infidelity with you" She seemed almost too happy with this statement, "Which brings me to the second contract you hold"

"Divorce?" The word stung my ears. I had never wanted to be named in anybody's legal separation.

"I couldn't be happier" She brushed aside the comment, "I would not have had you on this desk if I was in a secure relationship, and beside he has his harem of whores. He pretty much confessed to me that when he pushed you through the window he went home with at least two different girls"

She rose and walked around the desk. Her tight black top revealed her perfect body and I really wanted her again.

"So I have made a decision" She had now paused in front of me. Her hands were placed either side of my thighs and she leaned in closer. I could smell her toothpaste on her breath mixed with at least one cup of coffee as she spoke, "I have signed over the entire ownership of this business to you. That way he cannot take fifty percent"

"Wait... what?" I gasped.

"You now own this little gem" Her lips were almost touching mine, and then she pulled away, "For the time being. I mean after the divorce I want my shares back, and that is written in the contract"

"Done" I gulped. I was really turned on by now and I could tell that she noticed. I tried to resist but she was my ideal woman after Margot Drake. I pulled her in closer and before I knew it her tongue was darting into my mouth.

Then our clothes came off.

# The Light Of Friendship

We were interrupted when the telephone rang some time later, and whilst she took the call in the nude, I dressed back in my black ripped jeans and checked shirt and I refreshed myself in the bathroom. Things were really starting to look up and as I inspected the healing scratches on my body I thought briefly of Margot and then those words from the priest whispered in my ear about moving on.

"I think it's time" I whispered.

I made my way back into the office and Cassidy was now fully dressed although unkempt and she smiled.

"That was the confirmation I was waiting for" She grinned, "I leave in an hour"

"Leave?" I questioned like a gormless child.

"I never got to explain" She sighed. "Now that I am getting divorced I have nothing left in West Waterford, so I am going to travel the world and seek out international acts for Wild Wolf World. So keep your emails active because we're going global"

"You're leaving" I spoke with a hint of pain in my voice.

"You didn't think that I was going to stay?" She asked as she stepped closer toward me, "Lee, I love you but I cannot stay. If I did Jesse would make my life hell"

"Maybe I could come with you" I offered.

She touched me on the shoulder, "No"

She was so blunt with her rejection and I opted to shrug it off, "Well where are you starting off?"

"I am booked on a flight to Florida tomorrow morning" She replied.

With that she turned her back to me, and I tried not to look but it was so fine, I just wanted to grab it.

### 8 - Moving On.

That evening at home, I ordered a pizza and cracked open a few tins of cheap lager that I purchased from a nearby corner shop. My thoughts flashed between both Cassidy and Margot. Whilst I knew that Cassidy was travelling for some time, I wanted to believe that when she came back from her travels we could pick it up where we left off.

I dreamt about her that evening. We kissed passionately and rolled in the white sanded beach of some unknown destination and when I awoke I had a wet patch where my crotch lay. With a cheesy smile on my face I stripped the bed and leapt into the shower for the first time in a while. The murky grey water made me grimace a little as I used the last of my shampoo and conditioner.

I dressed in fresh clothes and I gave myself a look in the mirror as I brushed my hair into place.

I thought I heard a noise in my house. It sounded like someone was on the stairwell up to the first floor. I poked my head out of the bathroom which overlooked entrance. Although nobody was there, I heard the sound of a step creaking under the weight of a person again.

"Is anybody there?" I asked, and then giggled to myself because clearly there was not.

I was happy for many reasons and to top it off, I was about to see my friend Chris for the first time in a while and I brushed aside the noise.

\*\*\*

# The Light Of Friendship

Blakemore's Afternoon Delights was the hipsters dream coffee shop on the edge of West Waterford and it smelt of wood-shavings and caffeine as I entered. I was the only customer and the miserable barista with the dreads barely acknowledged me as I approached the counter. It almost seemed like I was an inconvenience for him as I ordered two lattes for both Chris and I.

I chose the two unmatched comfy chairs next to a roaring fireplace and Chris arrived just moments after the coffees were placed carelessly in front of me. He looked well, I could not even see a trace of bruising from my assault.

"I just wanted to apologise again for kicking you" I said before he even had the chance to say anything, I just wanted to say it out loud again.

He raised his hands as if to stop me, "Listen Lee, what is in the past remains where it should be. I am not here to listen to you ask for forgiveness because I have already accepted your apology. Tell me about you. Are you alright?"

What on Earth did I do to deserve such a good friend?

"It's been one of those where everything can either be up or down" I confessed, "Mostly down"

He did not say anything, and just listened.

"After I did what I did, I sank into a bit of a depression. When you called me I was about to slice my wrist but you stopped me. I admit that this was the longest week of my life waiting for you because I just felt so guilty..." I began.

"Stop" He smiled, and I knew that I was waffling.

"Just yesterday Cassidy gave me the entire business so that she doesn't have to give her soon to be ex-husband anything in their divorce" I continued, "We made love again and I really thought maybe it was time to move on from Margot"

He noticed that I paused.

"If you think that you are ready to move on you should" He offered.

# D T Lewis-Dayle

"She is leaving for Florida today" I bit my bottom lip, "She will be gone for some time"

"Could you possibly wait until she returns?" He pressed.

"I waited for over thirty years for someone like Margot to come into my life" I shrugged, "That priest told me I would know when it was time to meet someone new and start afresh"

"Perhaps that vicar speaks the truth" He suggested.

"Will Margot understand though?" I questioned.

"I think you know what to do" He smiled.

I sat in thought for a moment and sipped the sour tasting coffee that had already gone cold.

"Perhaps you should go to the airport?" He suggested, "If Cassidy makes you happy you should go get that trophy, because my mission in life is to ensure that you are smiling. I feel that she does that. You have your passport right?"

"I cannot just go chase her through Winchester Airport" I laughed.

"Why not?" He urged, "Taryn and I can look after your business until you come back?"

"Do you think I can do this?" I began to excited, checking the internet on the telephone, "The flight has been delayed. If I rush home for my passport I can just make it…."

"Why are you waiting?" He interrupted, almost as excited as I was.

"I'm going to do it" I squealed.


After I gave him the key and alarm code I raced home, ordering a cab on my way home. It was already there by the time I raced into my house. I retrieved my credit card and passport from the bedside cabinet and I did not even care that I had no clothes to pack.

## The Light Of Friendship

The ride to the airport was swift and I tipped the driver way too much but I needed to get into the terminal. I ran along the glass corridor, ignoring the moving floors that people opted for and I ran into the check-in.

Impatiently, I wait for the queue to decrease. Trust me to be caught behind an argumentative couple that blamed each other for their overweight baggage.

"I need to get on the next plane to Florida" I urgently requested as I reached the desk.

The bimbo behind the desk fumbled about on her computer for a while before returning with a well-rehearsed apologetic face, "I am sorry sir, there is no flight now until tomorrow"

"You mean that one this morning has been cancelled?" I sighed with relief.

"I am sorry" She chimed, "That flight was delayed but it took off about fifteen minutes ago...."

The rest of her words were drowned out with my own ignorance and I walked away with a heavy heart.

For the rest of the day I opted to return to Winchester City Centre and I drank myself into a stupor. It hurt so much that I had missed Cassidy by such a short time. I really wanted her to be the one that I spent the rest of my life with but now I knew that I had to wait until she returned. Whenever that would be.

I wasted the entire battery power on my mobile telephone just thinking of the words that I continually deleted on my message to her on social media. It never got sent.

I found a bar that was heaving with beautiful women and I believe that I was one of only a handful of men that were not staff. Although I despised myself I chose a flame haired girl that seemed to be alone and before I knew it we were grinding with a smile to some music that was not my type.

# D T Lewis-Dayle

     I awoke next to her the following morning and I quietly dressed and left her in the hotel room that I had paid for. I did not even remember her name as I caught the tram back to the train station. Through the rain stained windows of the train toward West Waterford I saw Margot again and once more she did not see me. She was standing alone at the opposite platform. My train started to move just as she boarded her own.

     I felt sick again and I allowed a tear to fall from my eye.

### 9 - Ghost Encounter.

Monday was a blustery day and I arrived at the same airport only this time I had a suitcase. I had chosen to travel in a comfortable jeans and tee-shirt combo. I wasn't sure that the same woman checked me in but I kept my head down and chose to sit in one of the lounges favouring a neat whisky and a plate of sandwiches from the buffet before my flight to Palma was announced.

I arrived in the Spanish sun shortly before 4pm, and I was met with a limousine to the nearby hotel. My room was basic but I did not care. I already knew that I was to meet Polly Anna and the rest of The Screaming Queens at a nightclub that had been hired out especially for the shoot later that evening. I had received confirmation that I was to dress as a Mafia boss, and I had chosen to dress in half black, half white outfit right down the middle. I knew that as I walked through the reception I was getting looks but I smiled as I was finally coming back to my former self.

My limousine collected me at midnight and as I entered the post-apocalyptic themed nightclub, I noticed the band had already set up on the central podium and Polly Anna sauntered over toward me.

"I'm liking the outfit" She stroked my arm, "Are you going to let me come back to yours tonight?"

"Keep your knickers on Polly Anna" I sighed, "This is strictly professional"

"What are you gay or something?" She questioned.

"Ask me when we're not on business" I smiled, "Which I believe is Wednesday evening"

# D T Lewis-Dayle

"Spoilsport" She laughed as she took my hand and led me toward the remaining band, "Perhaps in the next music video I would have just a pure sex scene and we can go full on method acting"

"Behave" I beamed, I have to admit she was definitely stirring something in the loins, maybe I would be an amateur and let her take advantage of the Napier loving after all.

"I understand that you grieve over the loss of your female" She purred, and although she had zero respect for Margot, she really was hot. I had no idea when Cassidy would be back so maybe I could revert back to the old Lee Napier and sleep with anyone with breasts and a pulse for a time?

"Perhaps you could venture back to my hotel room at some point?" I suggested. She knew where I was staying.

"I knew you were weak" She licked her lips as we finally made it to her team, "I will be on top of you before you know it you handsome beast"

She re-introduced me to the band that I already knew, and as she sat on one of the stools she flashed me proof that she was not actually wearing underwear with an overly simply leg cross and a knowing wink.

Tonight the music video of 'Mafia Run' saw the band playing a live rock tune as I shot my victim for an unpaid bill, and the make-up artist took most of the morning doing the gunshot wound. I spent most of the time either sitting with the band or flirting with Polly Anna in the designated smoking area. There was something about the way that Polly Anna would curl the smoke from her lips that made me weak and we ended up having an over-the-clothes fumble and kiss moments before we were called in to film the aftermath. This basically saw me ignore the patrons of the bar and leave into the amber sunrise.

# The Light Of Friendship

We finished that days recording at 7 in the morning and we were to be at another destination just after midnight again. Polly Anna chose to go home and I opted to grab myself a full-English breakfast from one of the taverns nearby. I felt tired from the whole night shoot and the scar on my leg tingled through the sweat and heat.

Being in Spain and having completed a whole 24 hours without sleep, I chose to enjoy one of the local beers rather than a coffee. I felt guilty as most holiday makers were not even awake and placing their towels on the sunbeds.

I chose to walk along the beach on the way back to the hotel soon after. The sun was already warm and although it was mid-June there did not seem to be many people around. I could see why people came this beautiful tiny island in the Atlantic. I became distracted by a group of beautiful young ladies that excitedly raced toward their spot on the beach, and one in particular stood out. She was set back slightly from the others making me believe that she was not part of that particular cluster. She wore a blue bikini and a matching sarong. The shades that covered her big blue eyes and an over-sized straw hat that covered her hair, but I knew that it was her straight away.

"Margot" I spoke as she brushed past me, the back of my hand gently touched her arm.

"Lee" Her mouth formed a perfect 'O'

"I have missed you" I stammered.

She clasped my hand and pulled me forward for the most passionate kiss that I had ever experienced. She groaned with ecstasy and the fact that she felt cold in this heat didn't go unnoticed.

"I tried to save you" I muttered into her lips between kisses.

"You were amazing that night" She gasped, "You sent them all running for their lives before it happened"

"It was over too fast" I cried, bringing her closer to me, I wanted to protect her more now.

"The funeral was beautiful" She agreed, "I walk there every day just to remember the service. I was so proud"

"I wanted it to be so special" I confessed, and she inched closed.

"It really was" She agreed, "I couldn't have planned anything better"

"It should have been a wedding instead" I felt like such a pathetic being, "I had the whole thing planned, from a Halloween wedding and a honeymoon in Brazil"

"You know that you were never any good at keeping a secret Scrumpy?" She giggled, "I was prepared for that all along. Your email password was so simple to crack"

"ScrumpyDoll" I recalled, "We can still go"

"How is Macy?" She enquired

"She ran away some time ago" I bowed my head.

"I never thought that I would see you again" She whispered, "I want to make love to you again"

I swallowed as I recalled what I had said to Polly Anna just hours before, and the fact that I was willing to move on with Cassidy recently. The guilt tore my heart and I knew that I had to come clean, and I spoke so fast that I was unsure she understood, "I was so faithful with you, and after the funeral I went into hibernation mode. I have slept with Cassidy a couple of times but she is gone. But Margot it is you that I love if you can forgive me?"

Her response stunned me, "I am here now and I don't care what happened in between"

I kissed her again.

"Take me home" She ran her hands down my back, and I felt that chill again.

# The Light Of Friendship

   I was in Heaven. Lying with her once more I felt complete. Her cool skin felt great in the increasing Mallorcian heat, and as I watched her breathing beside me, thoughts of how she could be here frightened me for a moment. But she was and I loved that I had my Baby Doll back.

   "Scrumpy" She moaned in her sleep, and then she whispered something nonsensical.

   I stroked her body, savouring every moment, "I am never leaving you again"

   I loved her scent, it was the perfect blend of her favourite soap and moisturiser along with the perfume that I purchased for her birthday.

   "Lee" She mumbled, and I embraced her in a spoon formation.

   "I love you" I kissed the back of her neck, and closed my eyes.


   I awoke some time later alone. She was gone again and I was in my own room. I knew that I could not have dreamt everything. I could smell her scent in the air.

   "Margot" I called out loud, before tailoring into a whisper, "Baby Doll"

## 10 – I Miss You.

I searched for her to no avail, and I spent the next two days filming the rest of the music video for The Screaming Queens and having meaningless sex with Polly Anna at any opportunity that presented itself. Afterwards I cried in the shower and scrubbed myself clean but yet I went back. I despised myself and each time I swore that I would not do it, but as I tired from not seeing Margot, I buckled. What kind of a man was I?

Polly Anna joined me in my limousine transfer back to the airport, and as I gathered my suitcase she wrapped her arms around me outside the terminal, "Can we pick this up back in West Waterford?"

"I don't know" I shrugged.

"So you're treating this like a holiday fling?" She seemed upset.

I nodded, and turned without speaking.

I arrived back in West Waterford shortly before noon the next day having stayed over in Winchester due to the time that my flight landed, and I called briefly into the office. Taryn and Chris were both busy on the telephone as I arrived and I made myself a coffee before joining them.

"You two seemed very active" I observed.

"Absolutely" Taryn grinned, "We have secured you some exciting gigs over the next few months and Tonia has lined up a massive gig in San Francisco for The Screaming Queens featuring someone called Lee Napier. You fly out next week"

She produced a print-out confirming an itinerary for next week.

# The Light Of Friendship

"We have already sorted out flights and visa requirements" She continued, "And of course we will be more than happy to stay on here"

"Wow" I was genuinely surprised because I was not expecting anything like this.

"Also, I had a meeting the other day with a director of a thriller that's being filmed in Scotland and also Germany" Chris waited for a moment for me to digest, "I think we spoke about this previously"

"The vampire one?" I could barely control my excitement.

He continued "I showed him your show reel and he liked what he saw and you will be filming in September"

"This is amazing" I was taken aback as he showed me the name Luke Sparrow on a script. I had heard of this man, he was a mid-thirties international horror director who had started out making short films for the internet when he was fifteen. He was married to a gorgeous burlesque model who went under the name Sambuca I had admired for years because of her assets and I had one of her posters at home.

"The role is Theo Brandt, he's a vampire from the Middle-Ages…." Chris surmised, but I had already read the synopsis of the script called 'Bite' in my mind and I loved it.

"Thank you" I almost cried again.

"There was a girl that visited yesterday" Taryn seemed cautious, and I could tell by the glance from Chris that he really did not want to talk about it.

"Who was it?" I queried.

Reluctantly, Chris turned the laptop security camera toward me and selected a file. As soon as it flickered to life, I saw Margot again.

"She wanted to talk to Cassidy" He explained, "But when we told her that she was away she simply said she would come back another time"

# D T Lewis-Dayle

My finger touched her face on the screen and my mouth opened slightly.

"Is everything alright?" Chris asked, and I nodded.

      I somehow ended up back at the church again. I had no idea how I arrived there and it was the sudden shower of rain that alerted me to my location. I sought shelter under the entrance from the downpour and my sleeveless tee-shirt stuck to my skin because I had left my jacket at home. I don't know how long that priest was there watching me, he startled me when he draped a towel around my shoulders.

"I thought I would see you again" He invited me inside.

I waited for a coffee and as he sat next to me I felt comfortable again. I had dried my long hair and I felt a mess but something about this visit felt settling.

"The last time we saw each other I told you about seeing Margot..." I began.

"I recollect" He nodded.

"I saw her again" I confessed, "We made love"

I could tell by his silence that secretly he was questioning me.

"It's impossible to make love to a ghost" I agreed, "But it was her. She smelled the same and she told me that the funeral was perfect. She understood that I had tried to move on with my business partner"

"My dear child, I have been a priest for many a year, but I have never heard of someone being intimate with a ghost" He shook his head, "I am not saying that you did not experience the relationship of your loved one. I don't believe it to be a possibility"

"It was like the first time" I recalled, "She was perfect"

# The Light Of Friendship

"Lee" He placed his hand on my knee, "In all sincerity, I do believe that you wanted to reconnect with Margot and somewhere in your subconscious you manifested a veil of familiarity with the one person that you loved in life. But your ghostly visions of her are not healthy"

"You are a man of God" I responded.

"Christ rose from the grave for our sins" He spoke as though he could read what I was about to say.

"Then why has Margot come back?" I questioned.

"When we had our last conversation, you explained that you believed it could be time to move on" He reminded me, "Perhaps part of you has since realised that it may not be the right time?"

Automatically, my head bobbed in agreements as I recounted the fact that Polly Anna and I had made out a few times at that nightclub and she rejected my offer to return to the hotel. I bought to mind that Margot was not actually with those other girls that I had seen that morning on the beach. Maybe the priest was right? I felt a tear fall down my face which I wiped with my finger.

"Why do I see her?" I queried, "The video footage picked her up at my business. Chris and Taryn saw her..."

"What did the woman in your office have to say?" He questioned, "Would there be a possibility that it was a girl that simply looked like your fiancé?"

"There is no sound on the video" I felt pathetic.

"Go home and play it back" He offered, "Look at her facial expressions and see if you can read what she is saying to your friends...."

Again, I nodded.

# D T Lewis-Dayle

"May I tell you something about my own life?" He spoke bringing me back to the moment. I noticed that he withdrew a wallet from his trouser pocket. He seemed to be smiling at something inside, and he continued without waiting for my permission, "My son James was twenty seven when he passed away. I was tending to his grave the day that we met if you remember"

"I am sorry to hear that" I nodded as I recalled our meeting. The priest presented me a photograph from a sleeve inside.

The grainy image was that of a teenage boy with blonde hair that beamed back at me.

"I guess that I am saying I have a personal interest in your grief process with Margot because my child's death was unexpected" He continued, "One day he was a happy young lad that was out celebrating life and that evening he went asleep and an undiagnosed     took him"

"He's a good looking lad" I found myself agreeing.

"I think he could be the double of your friend Chris" He accepted his photograph back, "Do you not agree?"

"It's uncanny" I bobbed my head in agreement, "It is almost like they could be related"

"My sons name wasn't Chris though" He sighed, "But when you showed me your own picture of you and your friend, I felt somewhat comforted...."

The office of Wild Wolf World was quiet as I entered, it was still light outside, but Chris and Taryn had left hours ago. I logged onto the computer and quickly located the footage. She was perfect as usual and it was certainly my Margot.

I touched the screen again, her face fitted perfectly to my finger and I watched her lips move, and "What are you saying?"

"I miss you" Her voice whispered in the darkness, startling me into a panic.

# The Light Of Friendship

I could not see her. I scanned the entire building twice. I even looked into the lockers just in case she was hiding in one.

"Margot" The tears were real this time.

"Lee" She responded after a moment silence, "I cannot go on like this anymore"

"I am here" I urged, "Talk to me"

I heard the door close behind me. I ran as quickly as I could to the entrance, and into the empty street beyond, calling her name.

Nonchalantly, I returned back to the same desk that I had just sat, and then I saw the ring and note precariously placed next to the keyboard.

# D T Lewis-Dayle

### 11 – The Cat Came Back.

I slammed the note and ring onto the desk so hard that both Taryn and Chris jumped at the sound, "Why didn't you pass me this when I came into the office yesterday?"

"We haven't seen that note before" They both protested in unison.

"Lies" I screamed, snatching the note back and reading it word for word, "I cannot continue living in West Waterford with the memories so I have chosen to leave once and for all. I will always miss you Scrumpy but the ring is a painful memory so I want to leave it behind"

"She never left anything as you have seen from the video" Taryn commanded the room now, "You walked off in tears because it disturbed you. If she had passed us something at the time we would have told you"

"Why did you come back here last night?" Chris pressed.

"I wanted to know what she said" I insisted.

"We told you before you left, she wanted to speak with Cassidy and when we told her that she was away she said she would come back" Chris reiterated and I remembered that this was pretty much what he had explained yesterday.

"She must have seen that I was here last night" I shrugged, "So she sought the opportunity to come into the office and leave this"

I sank back into my seat.

"I don't understand" I sighed after what seemed like an eternity, "I buried her with the ring. Does her ghost really not want to see me that she would just bring it back to me?"

They did not answer.

"I need a beer" I insisted and turned to Chris, "And a game of pool"

# The Light Of Friendship

We arranged to meet at Woodies later that afternoon, but prior to this I needed to trim my beard and have a shower to calm down. I chose to dress in black denim and a leather jacket and I sprayed my deodorant everywhere.

As I left my apartment I became aware that I was being watched from my own garden.

"Who is there?" I questioned.

I paused as I waited for the perpetrator to reveal themselves.

"I know someone is there" I insisted, "Come out now"

The rose bush to my left shook a little and braced myself.

"Now" I insisted.

My heart sank as I saw the blackened paw step out from beneath the greenery revealing Macy who sauntered toward me and ultimately snaking between my open legs before I lowered myself to her. She seemed standoffish a little before allowing me to stroke her gently.

"Where have you been?" I asked as picked her up. It certainly was her, I could tell by her affection, "Margot is going to be so...."

I stopped, and lowered myself to the ground, affectionately caressing the cat that had been missing for months.

"She is going to be so happy that you came home" I concluded my sentence as I snuggled into her soft fur.

Chris was already playing pool with someone as I arrived, so I took the opportunity to order us a couple of beers and I sat and watched them play for a short time. The bald opponent took the loss badly and walked off without as much as a thank you for the game. Chris went into auto-pilot mode and reset the game.

"You will never guess why I am late" I spoke before he could even answer, "Macy came back"

# D T Lewis-Dayle

"Your cat" Chris smiled, "They always come home eventually"

"I had given up on her" I confessed, "But she is now happily in her little basket by the radiator"

He offered me the cue to break. I took aim and I sank two red balls instantly. The fact that my cat had come back was certainly a piece of luck.

"Taryn was very upset with your confrontation earlier" Chris spoke as he watched.

I bowed my head, "I am sorry about that. I reacted badly"

"Perhaps you can apologise to her?" He suggested.

"Of course" I nodded and then I took another expert shot blocking his chance immediately, "I have a tendency to shoot from the lip when I am wrong"

"You are on a euphoric journey at the moment" He assured me with those simple words that he was not angry at me, "You have San Francisco to look forward to and the new movie and now Macy has returned, I guess things really are looking up for you"

"That reminds me" I was still waiting for him to take his game, and I snapped off a spare key from my bunch, "Will you look after Macy whilst I am away?"

"Yes" He accepted the key whilst working out how to take this next go, and then he expertly maneuvered out of the tight spot I had placed him in, and in return set up the perfect move to stop me from hitting a red. He then went on to type in a message on his phone, "I have asked Taryn to come along. She will be drinking a white wine spritzer...."

I obeyed and returned to the bar.

# The Light Of Friendship

Taryn arrived after five more games and Chris had won all of them. I actually hated him for being so good at a game that I prided myself in being an expert. The bar was unnaturally empty for the time of the day and the buxom barmaid joined Chris outside for a cigarette as I sat opposite the curly haired blonde woman.

"I know that this may sound cliché, but I really wanted to tell you how sorry I am for my behaviour yesterday" I apologised.

"Whilst I accept your expression of regret, you really hurt me with your accusations that Chris and I were hiding something from you" Her response was a little more harsh than I would have expected, "We have been working hard at Wild Wolf World on top of our own work and we really do not need to be screamed at by you"

"Understood" I was taken aback, "And I appreciate what you both are doing for me at the moment. You and Chris are the only ones that I can trust with everything"

"Well don't get used to it Lee" She snapped, "Chris and I won't be around forever, and I think really you should get used to it"

"You're leaving?" I questioned.

She sighed as she took my hand, "We need to get back to our own lives. Chris thinks the world of you. You literally are all he talks about at home. He doesn't have many friends, I would probably say that they are more like associates"

"I guess our friendship really is intense" I agreed, "He is always there whenever I need him"

"And yet you kicked him in the face a while ago" She reminded me causing me to recall that horrific night.

"He told me he forgave me for that" I offered.

"He may have forgiven you" She removed her hand from mine and took a sip of the spritzer, "But for me it is different. You cannot go around beating up someone that you call a comrade and expect butterflies, rainbows and unicorns delivering pizza. I understand that you have gone through a bad time recently and the ghost of your dead fiancé is haunting you but there has to be a line"

"What are you saying Taryn?" I asked.

"I think you need to loosen the reigns on Chris. Let him go" She shrugged, "I am happy for us to stay on and help you at Wild Wolf World for the interim. I am not saying we should leave straight away, but I truly believe that you should move on sooner rather than later"

As she concluded her words, I noticed that Chris and the barmaid had returned and were standing at the bar. She was pouring our next drinks.

I nodded, "May I set a target to work on this?"

"We really could do with being back home by the end of the year" She offered, "Please do that for him"

Before I could answer, Chris was already on his way back with the drinks.

"Ok" I whispered to her, "I will do this for my best friend"

Taryn greeted her boyfriend with a kiss.

"I take it everything is well?" He smiled.

"Lee was just telling me that he thinks he may be able to cope soon now that his cat is back" She grinned.

"Yes" I reluctantly agreed, although I had not spoken about Macy to her, I decided to hold back, and I bit my bottom lip as I took in what she had said.

## 12 – San Francisco.

I arrived in San Francisco on Friday ready for the gig. Polly Anna and the rest of The Screaming Queens had already been there for a few days to practice and set up and I was greeted by a limousine again that took me to my extravagant hotel which was way out of my budget in the steep Nob Hill. I giggled at the name in my head as I entered my room to rest after the journey.

I was awoken during the night as the telephone in my room rang so loud that it jolted me out of the deep sleep where I dreamt of all people Taryn and her confrontation.
"This is the reception" The voice spoke, "Your driver will be out front in fifteen minutes"
I thanked the receptionist and stepped into the shower for the quickest one ever before dressing in my vampire costume from 'The Creature of The Night' music video, and I did not bother with make-up as I knew that their special effects artist would be on site. I got a few strange looks as I stepped into both the elevator and the foyer. I was greeted by Franks, the same driver that had delivered me to the hotel.
"Sir" He opened the door for me.
I stepped inside, and smiled as I was offered a champagne flute.
"You took your time" Cassidy laughed as I sat next to her.
"Good to see you" I accepted the drink, and as Franks started to drive, I turned to her, "I tried to catch you at the airport you know"
"That was the strangest day" She agreed, "The flight was delayed indefinitely, and then all of a sudden we were called aboard and we were flying within half an hour"
"Did you hear what I said?" I asked.

D T Lewis-Dayle

"Why did you do that?" She queried.

"Because I thought that it was time to move on. I was willing to give everything up and travel with you" I confessed.

"You great big idiot" She took a sip of her drink, "I told you that I would come back when the time is right. Just let me travel and build up our portfolio for a year. Maybe two. I will always come back"

"Funny" I giggled and I explained that Macy had returned recently.

"Just give me that time I asked for" She purred as she rested her head onto my chest.

We chatted about everything we could possibly think of throughout the rest of the journey.

The Screaming Queens were the headline act and their fans had come from all over the world for this event. I signed autographs from fan-girls and boys who recognized me from the video that had been shown on television and social media networks. It felt amazing that people knew who I was.

The first act came to a crescendo of the live performance of the premier 'Mafia Run' combined with the film that we made in Mallorca and it was met with an overwhelming rapturous applause and pats on the back from the audience. I fought my way to the private bar that was reserved for just the band and its V.I.P members. Cassidy was at a table with the artiste's presumably chatting business as I stood next to a familiar looking blonde girl. I was so used to seeing Margot everywhere I looked now that I chose to ignore her at this particular moment.  She muttered something that I think that I was meant to hear but as I tried to track her again she had disappeared out of the tent. I continued to order an overly expensive beer and returned to the group.

# The Light Of Friendship

"Next stop is the world tour" Cassidy concluded her conversation just as I sat down, and she took my hand, "The band want you to play guitar for them in the live shows"

I hadn't played since the funeral, "I will brush up"

"Just the videos that you perform in" Polly Anna interrupted, "We cannot just give away the bass position"

"Perfectly understood" I sensed that she was still angry at me for abandoning her in Mallorca.

I barely had time to finish my two word sentence as the announcement was made that the band needed to return for the second act and they all started to disperse, and I took Polly Anna by the hand.

"You made your thoughts pretty clear" She hissed when she was aware that we were alone.

"I know that you are bored of hearing that I am the grieving party, but I just wanted to let you know that I am going to change" I confessed.

"Too late" She sighed, "I wasted my time chasing you Lee, and you simply were not worth it. You had a reputation of being the good time boy who always made his women happy just by having a big heart and making them feel comfortable"

"I will be that man again...." I began.

"And I will not be waiting" She rebutted, "You will always be that one that just wouldn't go anywhere, and I will remember you in years to come. However I have already met someone else"

I felt as though I had been punched but I deserved it. She deserved to be happy and deep down I knew that it was not meant to be me.

I watched as she walked out of the tent and I took a sip of my beer.

"You simply cannot keep it in your pants can you?" Cassidy grinned, I had no idea that she had returned.

"We didn't...." I stopped myself.

# D T Lewis-Dayle

She had placed her finger on my lips, "Take me back to the hotel"

We kissed pretty much the entire drive home, and poor old Franks had to listen to the wet smacking sounds. My mind was racing because whilst I really did want to apologise to Polly Anna. However right now, my tongue was in the back of the mouth of my good friend Cassidy. I really was becoming the man-slut that I used to be and then I thought for a moment that Margot was there with me. I almost weakened but then I found the strength to continue.

I awoke in my San Francisco bed alone as the sun rose outside. For a minute I believed that she had absconded after the night of passionate love-making that we had just experienced and I would truly deserve it. My mind rested as I heard the shower running nearby and I could tell by her silky tones that Cassidy was still here.

I then smelt it again. The perfume that I had purchased for Margot. It lingered onto my nostril hair and I panicked inside. I dressed in the same clothes that I had worn previously and raced over to the balcony just to escape the familiarity.

"I am sorry" I whispered, "I shouldn't have done that"

I turned back and smiled cautiously as Cassidy meandered into the room with my hotel issue dressing gown on.

"You coming back to bed?" She invited.

I swallowed and nodded and returned my gaze to the city scape before me.

"Forgive me" I mouthed.

# The Light Of Friendship

## 13 – Taryn's Request.

Although Cassidy left that same morning for the next part of her journey, I wallowed in self-pity for the next four days until my flight home. If I was not having a meeting with the band in which Polly Anna would deliberately ignore me, I did the typical tourist experiences, such as The Golden Gate Bridge, Alcatraz and Lombard Street, but being on my own it was difficult to trust someone to capture the moment on my phone.

I slept all the way home and Macy welcomed me with a loud me-ow and she curled up on my lap as I fell asleep again on the couch.

It was a warm August afternoon and Wild Wolf World felt quiet without Chris or Taryn when I returned the following morning, but I was elated when I saw the number of event bookings in the diary and I felt grateful for them running the place in my absence.

I replayed the video footage of Taryn a few more times before I opted to work. It gave me some sort of comfort because other than the framed picture by my side, I had no idea where she was.

Eventually the phone rang, startling out oy own thoughts.

"Hullo, Lee speaking…." I did not realise how grumpy I must have sounded, and I listened to the query with a couple of occasional sounds of agreement and understanding, "That sounds like something we can do, I will send over an invoice shortly and that will need to be paid 28 days before the performance. So just to confirm the date again?"

"January 13th" The voice advised, I froze as I repeated it, marking it onto the calendar.

"Done" I controlled my emotion and closed the call.

# D T Lewis-Dayle

I realised that I was allowing that tear fall again. January 12<sup>th</sup> was the day Margot and I got engaged, and she died the next morning in a snowy roadside in my arms. I had enough for the day. I recorded a new voice message and shut up shop once more.

I leapt onto the first train out of town and I did not care where I was going. I had purchased some tins of cheap lager from an off licence that was open on the way to the station and I had finished them before we pulled up at the final destination of Middleton.

I had never been to the Industrial City in all my life so I had no idea where I was going so I just followed a group of lads that seemed to be out on a day drinking session. I stayed enough distance behind them so that they did not suspect that I was tailing them, and then I lost them as we reached a row of pubs and I chose the first. It was a 'trying to be modern old style bar' which was hosted by a flat-cap wearing elderly man and a girl young enough to be his granddaughter.

She took a shine to me and I allowed her to flirt but although I knew that it would not venture anywhere other than a playful smooch, I allowed her to take me to a few different venues after her shift. Her name was Lucy and at nineteen I felt like a lecherous old man for a moment until she made the move for a kiss.

\*\*\*

# The Light Of Friendship

We ended up in an underground night-club where the music was not at all to my liking and as the night drew on, Lucy met another man and slinked off into the smoking area with him and I nursed my beer at the bar. I had not planned on where I was going to stay for the night and then I recalled Chris and Taryn lived somewhere in Middleton. I found his number to call but stopped as I noticed that it was fast approaching midnight. Instead, I opted to use the internet to find a local hotel.

I really did not want to be alone tonight, but none of the women here were my Margot, and they weren't even a patch on Cassidy, or Polly Anna.

I eventually checked into a room above a bar nearby which was only a few minutes' walk away from the hell-hole I had been dancing like a maniac in. It was a basic bedsit style room with a sink with a dripping tap literally at the base of my bed, and a toilet that stunk of raw sewerage but I was too tired and drunk to even care.

I was awoken by a cacophony of dustbin men, nature and sirens outside just after sun-up. I had barely slept on this rock solid mattress and despite the warm weather I was cold. I chose not to shower or seek the breakfast and walked out of the room. The elongated corridor led to a steep staircase that made me think how on Earth did I climb that mountain last night?

# D T Lewis-Dayle

As I closed the gate into the back street, narrowly avoiding the dog turd that was created by some sort of gigantic beast, I allowed my eyes to adjust to the sunlight. I had managed to note on my mobile that it was barely even 05.30 as the battery cut out entirely and I knew that I was not going to get a charge until I made it home. I stepped over some bin bags that blocked the entrance to the cobbled road and I caught the attention of a passer-by on the other side of the road.

"You can't go that way mate" He called, "The police have cordoned off the whole area"

"What's happened?" I enquired.

"Dunno" He shrugged.

I glanced down the road and could see the blue lights flashing just on the horizon. My curiosity got the better of me and I opted to walk toward it with the intention that I was a stranger in the neighbourhood and lost.

As I neared the incident, I could that a white tent had been pitched on a grass verge. I had seen many crime documentaries to know that there was a body in there. For a moment I flashed back to that January night.

I had now become a complete stop and my attention was drawn toward the sound of footsteps to my left. I turned and I saw the curly haired woman walking away from me.

"Taryn?" I called out.

She stopped and turned. Startled she began to run.

"Wait" I called after her and took chase into the open field beyond the railings. She tried to outrun me, and I gathered pace before clasping at her arm.

"What are you doing here?" She panicked.

Suddenly, I became aware that she must have been there for a reason and I briefly turned to see the tent again, "Please tell me that nothing has happened to Chris?"

# The Light Of Friendship

She began to shake uncontrollably, and as I went to comfort her, I noticed that her hands were decorated with blood.

"Oh my God" I gasped, "It is Chris isn't it?"

"You don't know what you have done" She cried and I could sense the fear in her tone.

"Is this his blood?" I was beginning to freak out, thinking of my Margot, part of me wanted to scream out to the police nearby that I had apprehended the murderer.

"It's not him" She cried, "But you have to leave"

"Whose blood is it?" I pressed.

"None of your business" She wept, wiping away a dribble of snot from her nose, "Now please go back to West Waterford and forget that you have seen me...."

"You have just walked away from the scene of a crime and you expect me to forget?" I argued.

"Lee, you have just opened up Pandora's Box and Chris is going to need you more than ever now" She seemed frightened as she took my hands in hers, "He loves you like a brother. He sees you as his best friend and he is risking everything possible to be at your beckon call"

"I don't understand" I became aware that the wind was beginning to pick up, and a pendulous dark cloud was already forming.

"He will come to you tomorrow" She promised, "Just don't let him quit his mission"

"His mission?" I had suddenly become some sort of parrot and I chose to ignore the rain that started light but was now becoming more-heavier by the second.

"Go home" She urged again, "Chris is going to be an emotional wreck and you need to allow him to cry on your shoulder this time Lee. Like the time you called him and he met you in the graveyard. Be there for him"

# D T Lewis-Dayle

"Why, what is happening?" I called out aware that the rain was beginning to drown out my words.

She had let go of my hands, "You cannot tell him what happened…. Just promise that you will be there for him and if he tells you it's time, go with him…."

I barely had time to respond as a bolt of lightning flashed all around us.

"Taryn" I yelled, as she started to vanish in the torrential rain.

I opted to take chase again, but before I could move a second flash of lightening tore through the skies and hit something just outside of my vision.  The force of which sent me to the ground and I could smell smoke and no sooner as I rose to my feet again the storm seemed to subside just as quickly as it had come.

### 14 – The Masked Saviour.

The flash storm did not bother me but I could not shake Taryn's behaviour as I travelled home to West Waterford. Part of me despised her for lying to my best friend but I had ran around that park looking for her for at least an hour before I chose to leave. She had simply disappeared and I could not tell which exit she would have taken.

Macy was her impatient usual self and watched me as I showered and when I wrapped myself in my toweled dressing gown she curled up on my lap. I glanced at my telephone that was on the charging portal nearby and I smiled as I saw that I had received a voicemail. I knew that it would be him before I even pressed the button.

What sounded like static electricity whispered through my ear for a moment before he sniffled, "Lee, I really could do with someone to talk to. May I come around?"

"Sure" I typed my response, "I am here whenever you need me"

As I replaced the phone, I recalled again Taryn's words 'You need to allow him to cry on your shoulder this time'

He arrived in the early evening and he seemed a shadow of his former self. He had been crying and his eyes and cheeks were reddened. I did not want to press him so I simply held him in a cuddle for a moment in the middle of my lounge until Macy chose to inform us that she did not want to be with us. She began to Me-ow loudly signaling that she wanted me to open the door, and off she bounded into the bushes.

As I returned, I offered him a bottle of beer, and sat opposite him, "Are you alright?"

He did not answer instantly and I nodded as he sat uncommunicatively.

# D T Lewis-Dayle

"I will put on a movie and when you are ready to talk...." I suggested.

He nodded and I switched on the television.

The silence lasted an eternity. Every time that I raised a subject he simply grunted a single syllable response and several beers in, I wanted to push him. However I recalled how patient he was with me when he came to me that night in the cemetery.

The film finished and he excused himself to use the bathroom and I took the opportunity to grab us more alcohol from the fridge. When I returned he was weeping again.

"Please talk to me brother" My heart seemed to melt.

"Taryn is gone" He sobbed.

"Gone where?" I knew that Taryn had asked me not to tell him that I had seen him. But if push came to a shove I would tell him everything.

"She's been banished" He seemed to panic over his statement and quickly tried to retract, "She has taken a transfer"

I knew what I had heard, "What do you mean?"

"She was asked to cover another area and she took it this morning" He lied through his tears.

"Are you going to be with her?" I queried.

He shook his head, "It's impossible"

"How is that?" I asked, "Where is the secondment?"

"The other side of the world" He brushed away a tear, "I came home this morning and she was gone. I got a simple note saying goodbye"

I had seen his fiancé only hours before and I mistakenly believed she could have hurt my best friend, but he was lying to me. If Margot left me when she was still alive, I would certainly be able to track her down in a heartbeat.

# The Light Of Friendship

"What are you not telling me?" I spoke. It shocked me that I was so blunt with him.

"You have full disclosure on me and know everything about me" He responded, "There is nothing I can hide from you"

"I don't understand why you cannot be with Taryn any more" I replied.

After a long moment he sighed, "With our job, once you move on, you don't come back"

"Oh come on Chris, I don't mean to sound rude but you are a talent agent" I laughed which may have come across a bit curt to him.

"That's just the pinnacle of it" He seemed offended, "Why are you being like this?"

"I am sorry" I took a step back. I could not hurt him, "I am being insensitive. I just honestly don't understand what is happening to you"

"I forgive you" He apologised to me as he rose to leave, "I appreciate that you have never had a friend that you can talk to about your problems with. I am sorry to be an inconvenience"

"I didn't mean that" It was my turn to say sorry, "Please Chris, listen to me...."

"No" He stopped me as I approached him, "Think nothing of the fact that I dropped everything to come to you when you called me. I will once more excuse you and if you need me, I will be there because that's just what I do, now if you don't mind, I will take my leave...."

"What did Taryn mean when she told me that you should not quit your mission and that you are risking everything for me?" I blurted out. I did not want him to leave.

"I beg your pardon?" He stopped in his steps.

# D T Lewis-Dayle

I confessed everything to him. I told him that I had seen Taryn in the park and recreated the conversation as best I could. I even told him how I initially thought that she had hurt him because of the blood on her hands. To my surprise he listened and he somehow guided me back to the couch during the whole incident. I genuinely did not want him to go.

"I was aware that there was an accident this morning near our house and being a first aider, Taryn would have helped out at the scene until she was allowed to leave" He explained, I wanted to question this but I felt as though I would push him away. He continued, "Do you trust in me?"

"Yes" I confessed. It was true this man knew me more than any one of my closest friends.

"I know that you saw her earlier" He bowed his head, "I just miss her"

I inched closer to him, and placed my hand on his shoulder and I braced myself as I repeated again, "What did she mean with what she told me? About you risking everything and something about a mission?"

"I am not risking anything by being with my friend" He insisted almost defiantly.

"You're not telling me something" I soothed as I took his head into my chest.

He raised his head and a tear spilled as he spoke, "I knew who you were from the day that we met on the music video. At that very moment I passed you a coffee I believed that we would be firm friends and I did not expect you to become the best one I ever had. I heard you name mentioned only once before we met and I knew from your eyes alone that you were him. It was only when you spoke that I knew for certain"

"You knew who I was?" I could tell from his demeanor that he wanted to stop, but I wanted to him to explain. Without speaking he pulled away a little.

## The Light Of Friendship

He used the sleeve of his coat to wipe the tear and reached into his pocket, withdrawing a plastic wallet with a news article inside. He held it close to him for a moment before he spoke, "I almost turned down the extras gig on the video, but my agent sent me the call sheet and when I saw your name I felt like it was fate bringing us together again"

"Again?" I repeated that word like it was an echo but from another source.

I accepted the gift, and carefully unfolded the newspaper article, which showed a young Chris outside a court

The headline read, '*Victim thanks mysterious masked avior*'

"Eight years ago, in Winchester" He spoke as my eyes danced across the words, "I was almost killed when I was crossing a road and you bumped into me...."

The rest of his words were drowned out as several words jumped out at me, and I dropped the clipping to the ground placing my own head into my hands, shaking with fear.

# D T Lewis-Dayle

## 15 – The Story of Jack and Lee.

Eight years ago, I was fresh out of work and probably another doomed romance, and because I was unable to keep up with the rent I resorted to crashing at my good pal, Tommy Basford's bedsit in a slum just outside of Winchester. I stayed there with him and his wife until the day that he got arrested for ABH on her. I could never forget the day when the police kicked down his door and I almost spilled my cornflakes through fear. As they arrested him I could see a bruised and battered spouse that ordered me out of the house as soon as possible. That was when I met their next-door neighbour Jack Stephens.

He was a bit of a tramp that smelt of weed and cheap beer but I liked his sense of humour of fart jokes and minor sexism. Albeit a crummy mattress, at least at his home I had a bed.

I knew that he was a misfit but at the time I presumed that he was misunderstood.

In time I managed to secure a job at a bar called The Jester which was a rough council estate bar that saw more fights than I served beers and the landlady, Barb was a middle-aged hooker that dressed far too young than her sagging breasts should really allow her to. I liked Barb but it amazed me how many young gentlemen would cross her bedroom, even Jack enjoyed it on benefit day. She tried it on with me on many occasions but I simply turned her down with an excuse of impotence. I was unsure if I should be hurt by the fact she believed it.

## The Light Of Friendship

It was a Sunday lunch time when it happened. Just the day before Jack was panicking about money. I gave him what I could afford but it seemed to be passed back over the same bar and I had already resorted to lying to him about how much I was being paid just to save enough to move on.

"How much do you recon The Jester place is taking a night?" He whispered as he took a puff of his cigarette in the battered old bus-shelter that doubled up as a smoking area.

I knew what he was getting at and responded with a simple shrug.

"Tomorrow night" He smiled, "You and me brother"

"I don't like this" I responded.

"I've been casing the joint out for weeks" He explained, "Tomorrow lunch time will be quiet, just Barb and that regular old gimp that sits in the corner all day. The guy who comes to take the money out of the machines comes at 12.30 sharp"

He really had done his homework, and I listened.

"I have some Hallowe'en masks in a box under the kitchen sink. We will knock him out on the way in and then do the place over" He seemed like an excited teenager about to get his first hand-job.

"I don't want to be part of this" I insisted.

"You don't have a choice Lee" He spat, "Otherwise you will be sleeping on the streets my friend"

He had a point, it was March and cold and I suppose the mask would keep me hidden.

"So I can count on you?" He questioned.

"Yes" I nodded.

I barely slept that evening and when I entered the kitchen I was greeted by Jack and his creepy looking Goblin masks and a cup of weak coffee.

# D T Lewis-Dayle

He had arranged to loan a car during the night and we made our way to the heap of rust that resembled a Volkswagen Beetle, and then we waited in the car park just outside the bar, in our masks.

Like clockwork, the gambling machine driver arrived just before 12.30 and Jack raced over to him with a crowbar, slamming him over the head several times and obtaining his keys and safe. Nervously I stepped out of the vehicle just in time to stop him from killing the defenseless man. Together we walked into The Jester and he smashed the security camera with the same weapon that he had just used.

"All the takings now" He commanded as he approached Barb at the bar.

She obeyed as though it was a regular occurrence and I hovered by the old man in the corner to ensure that he didn't use his mobile or anything.

It was over that quick, and before I knew it we were running back out to the car.

"How much do you think we got?" I enquired through adrenalin, checking the heavy bag of coins that I had in my lap.

Jack didn't answer me as he pressed his foot on the accelerator and drove toward the exit.

I rose my head just in time to see a teenage blond male, concentrating too hard on his mobile, "Watch out"

Jack swerved to avoid the man.

"Let me out" I commanded.

"If I stop you don't come back" He hissed.

"Stop the car" I insisted.

He obeyed and stared forward as I pushed open the door, I did not turn back.

The shaken young fellow must have been clipped by the wing mirror as he sat on the ground cradling his elbow, and I rushed over toward him.

# The Light Of Friendship

"Are you alright?" I enquired, with my mask still covering my face, only my baby blue eyes were visible to him, "I tried to get him to stop"

I could tell that he was in pain and I wanted to make sure that this innocent bystander was safe.

He did not have time to respond as I heard the sirens in the distance and I opted to run leaving him injured on the roadside.

"I fled town that day and ended up here" I concluded, "I cannot believe that you were the teenager that he nearly hit with the car"

"Fractured elbow said otherwise" He smiled.

"You said that you knew my name and recognised it…." I was confused.

"Jack was trapped in the car and was arrested on site" He shrugged, "I was called to court as a witness and your name was mentioned once, so when I read your name on that sheet I knew that I had to meet you"

"That's why he attacked me and killed my Baby Doll" I surmised, "I knew when he initially came to West Waterford something was wrong but I got him an apartment and he seemed to be settling down. He even took that job in Australia…."

"He was probably plotting the right time to confront you" Chris offered.

"By taking the one thing that I loved" I agreed.

"I didn't think about you until just before we met last year" He continued, "I guess your name was always there in the back of my head and it was just coincidence that we were drawn together"

He was right. Two friends came into each-other's lives at the right time.

# D T Lewis-Dayle

"Let's forget about the past now" Chris held out his hand for me to shake, "Neither of us live there anymore, so let us both walk forward"

I nodded.

"Would you mind if I stay here for a while?" He asked, "Just until I get my head together?"

"Of course" I was happy for the company, "You can feed Macy when I am away next month"

"Deal" He agreed, "Pool?"

"I will get my coat" I grinned.

Woodies was busier than usual as we arrived and people were in fancy dress for some reason. We played several games of pool to which he won as usual but I did not mind. The fact that my best friend now had a smile on his face despite his woman troubles meant so much to me. As long as he was happy then the world was a better place for all.

# The Light Of Friendship

## 16 – The Return of Baby Doll.

Having Chris as a colleague and roommate was perfect especially as Macy loved him as much as I did. I often would come home from work and they would be curled up on the couch watching some terrible television. He was a great cook too. Taryn certainly was missing out on this. It bothered me a little that he never spoke about her almost as though he had forgotten her, and when I did broach the subject he would simply brush it off.

We celebrated his birthday on September 1st with a party at Woodies with friends. I had never really met any of his, but they all were of similar age and they seemed to enjoy themselves and he seemed close to a sweet looking girl that he had introduced as Susan, and for once I managed to win a game of pool during one of his inebriated states. I did not let this go to my head but I did plan on using it in a future comment.
I felt a weird sensation slice through my left thigh and subconsciously I stroked the scar again. It was beginning to hurt a lot more, and I made a note to inspect it when I had a moment.
Chris and Susan disappeared soon after midnight holding hands and I kind of felt pleased that he had managed to move on a lot quicker than I was. I took a moment to sit back and enjoy the party, but as they dispersed, I once more felt alone.

I was the last to leave and as I avoided the spot where Margot was murdered I felt as though I was being watched. I slowed down my pace and came to a complete stop before cautiously scanning the area.

## D T Lewis-Dayle

The sense of stillness felt somewhat comforting but as a trained martial artist I was aware that someone was certainly hidden in the natural darkness.

"I know you're there" I spoke.

I heard the rustle of clothes and as I turned I noticed a silhouette emerge from the shadows near to the bar.

"I came back" She spoke.

"Baby Doll" I was shocked as she stepped into the natural moonlight, "You're really here"

"I never really left Scrumpy" She took my hands in hers and bought me closer for an embrace.

"The note" I recalled, "You said you could no longer live in West Waterford"

She bit her bottom lip, "I spent a few weeks at my sisters but I had to come back for you"

I kissed her on the mouth again and savoured every second of it as my hands wandered down her back.

"I never want you to leave me again" She sighed as she pulled away, still holding my hands.

"Promise" I wanted to be kissing her again.

I lowered myself to my knee, and smiled, "I will always be by your side Baby Doll"

"Get up you big idiot" She giggled, and guided my lips to hers again, "I feel so lonely without you by my side….

She took control and led me back towards the home we once shared.

As we entered the apartment, Macy made a fuss of her mother and I made her favourite hot chocolate with milk boiled in a pan on the cooker. I could sense that we were alone and Chris had opted to spend the night with Susan. I once more silently thanked him and as I returned to the lounge, I smiled as Macy glanced up to me as if to say thank you for bringing her home.

# The Light Of Friendship

"She missed you more than me" I confessed.

"Charming" She jokingly jabbed me in the ribs as she sipped her drink.

I forcefully moved the beverage away from her, and slammed it onto the coffee table before kissing her, "Let's go to bed...."

We made love for almost an hour. Our lips barely left our flesh as we kissed almost every square inch of our bodies, and she held on tightly to me as though she feared I would vanish.

I became the big spoon as we clasped each other, and I nuzzled into the back of her neck.

I glanced down at our entwining physique, and I caught my wound on my thigh. It seemed angry, and I took an opportunity to gently rub the scar which seemed to soothe it a little as I recalled that horrific night as the knife loomed in the air whilst I round-housed my assailant sending him to the ground. It felt so real again and I watched as Jack slinked into the darkness and I erased the moment from memory what happened next. I never wanted to see her bleeding corpse before me again, there was no way that I could live through that another time.

"Why did you leave me that night in Mallorca?" I decided that my thoughts were too dark and I wanted to reconnect with my lover.

She shuffled and turned to face me, "I didn't leave you"

"When I woke up in my room, I could smell that perfume that I bought you...." I smiled.

"Lee" She interrupted, "When I saw you on that beach, I thought that I was in Heaven. It felt perfect that you were there. But when I awoke, it was you that had disappeared"

"No" I protested, I remembered specifically that we had gone to her hotel and not mine.

## D T Lewis-Dayle

"Because we made love, I slept soundly that night for the first time since the funeral" She seemed defensive, "You weren't there when I opened my eyes. There was no trace whatsoever of you ever being there Lee"

She had moved away and her legs were now swung over the edge of the bed, I reached over to stroke her back and she flinched.

"Why did you leave me?" She questioned.

I opened my mouth to answer but nothing came out. I knew for a fact that I had spent the night with her but somehow ended up back in my own room. I could not gage what happened.

She was now dressing.

"Stop, please" I pleaded, "I don't know what happened in Mallorca...."

"The day we got engaged you made a vow that you would never leave me" She muttered, "And yet you did"

"Baby Doll..." I began.

"Lee, you left me twice" She continued, "I thought that I was stronger than this, but I cannot handle you abandoning me again. I don't think I should have ever come back here"

"Margot, wait...." I stumbled out of the bed that we had just shared and started to dress.

She walked away from the bedroom, and I took chase calling her name. She chose to ignore me as she made her way back down the stairs and used her own key to open the door before entering the street beyond.

I struggled to get my leg into my jeans and I grabbed my shirt, "Baby Doll don't leave me again, I thought we were going to stay together..."

I slipped and tumbled down the entire flight of steps and blackness followed.

## The Light Of Friendship

I awoke in a private cubicle in a hospital some time later, and Chris was next to me reading a battered old novel that he had obviously found on one of the bookshelves.

"Margot..." I croaked.

He took my hand, "I am so sorry that I left you last night, I should have stayed"

"I lost her again" I felt myself cry again.

"How much did you have to drink?" He questioned, "When I got home, you were unconscious behind the door, you must have fallen down the stairs. What if I couldn't get to you?"

"Chris" I assured, "I had the most wonderful evening. Margot came home with me and we made love...."

"Why didn't she stay with you?" He queried.

"Because I am Lee Napier" I cried, "The stupid idiot who puts his foot in his mouth every time that he opens it...."

# D T Lewis-Dayle

## 17 - Bite

I was released from hospital a few days later into the care of Chris who listened to me go on about Margot. Although I believe that I must have bored him with my constant whining about my lost love, he played along and dutifully nodded and made me a coffee or a sandwich. I reverted back to hating myself for putting upon my best friend.

"Just concentrate on what happens next" He would often smile at me, and I agreed that looking forward was the best.

Just a few days later, I boarded the train to head to Scotland to meet Luke Sparrow the international horror film director. I recognised him immediately as I disembarked. He was a tall balding ginger man in a white suit, shades and a cigarette, and attached to him was a voluptuous younger model that I know instantly as Sambuca. I struggled for a moment to avert my eyes from her assets.

"So this is Theo?" He greeted me like an old friend as he referred to my character in the movie, "Little bit skinner than I would have liked but you come highly recommended"

"I think he's a perfect specimen" Sambuca purred as she stroked her husband's arm. I noted that she licked her lips a little and I could sense that she was flirting with both of us at the same time. She continued, "Much better than the Hollywood A-Lister you wanted…."

"He cost too much" I could not help but feel a little disheartened with this guys' words, "I take it that you have memorised my script by heart?"

"Most of it" I confessed, although I secretly had not even glanced at it in weeks.

# The Light Of Friendship

"Right then" He gestured for me to follow them, "We have an early start in the morning, I want to be on-set before sunrise for your opening scene…."

As I followed my new director, I watched the curvatious movements of his sexy wife who looked back with a knowing smile.

His mansion was situated deep in a wooded area very similar to those kind of films where teenagers venture to before being hunted down by inbreeds. However I was soon assured that there was only the three of us there with twenty-four hour security on the perimeters. It also did not surprise me that there was no mobile reception deep within the dense forest.

"So what do you think of your role as Theo Brandt?" Luke questioned as he poured a dangerous measure of gin and lemonade.

Luckily I remembered everything that I could, "I think I can do him justice. I was thinking of sporting a scar on his face to give him character…"

"No" He knocked the idea instantly on the head, "How can someone with a great dirty gash on his face be seen as the attractive bit of rough for the lead lady? And while we are at it, I do hope that you are going to shave that bush off your chin"

"I don't know Luke" His wife responded as she played on the grand piano casually, "The vampires of the modern genre beautify the creature of the night. Perhaps if we made the beast a loveable hero we can target a whole new audience…."

"Sex sells" Luke offered me the drink finally, "The monster must be perfect on the eye. I want a smooth, flawless face. I want the viewer to fancy Theo Brandt. The men would want to be like him and the girls will want to bed him…."

## D T Lewis-Dayle

"I think I am pretty good looking" I protested a little, and I could sense the cheeky grin from Sambuca despite the fact that she was facing away from me, "My character in the music video was a day walking vampire which defeats conventional mythology. Perhaps we should ask the actress who is playing the love interest for her opinion...."

"That will be me" Sambuca stopped playing the instrument with a sparkle that glistened in her eye. She sauntered from the stool and rested on a chair next to mine. I felt her hand wander up my thigh as Luke either remained ignorant to his wife's behaviour, or he simply did not care. She made me feel uncomfortable but I also kind of liked it, "I think that Lee Napier is perfect just the way he is, and his interpretation of Theo Brandt will be epic"

I adjusted my sitting position to move her away from me and I spotted a wry smile cross her face.

I stepped outside under the guise of a cigarette at the first opportunity. We had already read through some of the script a few times and it was decided that I would remain the 'piece of rough' that Sambuca wanted.

The night air was perfectly clear and I stared up into the skies. I spotted my star immediately and I remembered the night that Chris gave me the deed clearly. It was almost like his voice was whispering in my ear.

"Don't tell me you believe in aliens too" She spoke as she seduced me from the patio door, I could see that Luke was already asleep on the couch as she took several steps toward me, "He will be out until sun-rise now and we can have a little fun..."

I decided to change the subject, and I gestured upwards, "My pal bought me that star...."

"Is your friend after you?" She had reached me now and her hand was already touching my chest.

# The Light Of Friendship

"It would not bother me if he was gay" I defended him,
"He's my best friend"

"Whatever" She sighed, and she lowered herself, unzipping
my fly as she did so, "Stop talking about your friend"

"He's not though...he will always be my..." I did not finish
my sentence.

Three minutes and half a cigarette later, she smiled as
she wandered back toward the mansion, and I dressed myself.
I looked back up at the stars and I allowed a grin to tear across
my face.

The following morning we drove from the Sparrow
home to the location which was a cavernous area nearby deep
within the countryside. I did not see a single living person for
over an hour during that drive until we pulled into a carpark
that boasted a small tourist shop and a boating lake.

Luke introduced me to the make-up artist Jacqui, a petite
bespectacled lady with a paint brush in the bun at the back of
her hair bun. She reminded me a little of a cartoon character.

"I will be in caravan four for the next hour" She commented
after she inspected me for what seemed like an eternity, "You
only need a light base and fangs. Easiest project yet..."

With that she marched away to another group of people
that by the way that they were dressed they were to be my
victims from the Middle-Ages.

"Did you enjoy my wife last night?" Luke spoke from behind
me, startling me a little.

I stammered.

"That is the thing when you marry such a thing of beauty"
He sighed, "You cannot hold onto it by yourself, sometimes
her libido lets her take a new lover from time to time...."

"And you just let this happen?" I questioned.

# D T Lewis-Dayle

"Infidelity means nothing to me" He placed his hand on my shoulder, "We have an agreement in place. We are both allowed to stray whenever we want. However if she is to leave me then she would have nothing. I made sure of that in the pre-nuptial agreement she signed the day that we married"
"How can you be like that?" I asked.
"I'm rich and I can do what I want" He retaliated, "I believe that Jacqui needs you...."

I loved filming, especially movies. I loved it when a beautiful woman would cling onto me and I could chose to deliberately make the scene last longer or fly by as fast as possible. Sambuca was different. She was trapped in a loveless marriage to a millionaire and I knew that I was going to enjoy every moment of it.
The scene that I was about to shoot involved lots of on screen kissing and groping in front of the man that she had taken vows with. With my past with Cassidy I would not wish to embark on an affair with a married woman, but I could tell that Luke was a lot different than the monster that was Jesse.
"Action" The director called from his chair.
I seized the opportunity to act, I paced forward with a hint of anger in me and as I reached the love interest, I took her by the waist and forced her into me. Our lips met and I allowed my tongue to enter her mouth.

Filming took eight weeks in an endless stream of flights to and from Germany and on the final day, my on screen death was filmed on a stormy morning which added to the effect. Sambuca straddled me with pride as my lover stabbed me in the chest with a fake stake.
That evening we recreated the scene in my hotel bedroom for her pleasure.
I knew that she was falling for me, like I was her.

## The Light Of Friendship

"Let's run away together after this" I whispered.
"Yes" She purred.

# D T Lewis-Dayle

### 18 – The Raging Ravine.

Sambuca had the departure planned. She did not care about the money. All she wanted was me and we had decided to leave the day after the wrap party which had been held at a luxurious golf club. Luke was away filming scenes that I was not required for, and whilst I had already booked our flight to Denpasar in Bali and she had secured our getaway driver to take us during the night. I knew the evening itself would be hurtful as it was that bittersweet date of January 12$^{th}$, a year to the day that I proposed to my Baby Doll.

January 11$^{th}$ arrived in no time, and I watched the flurries of snow from my bedroom window. I could see my lover across the courtyard in her own room with her husband. It did not bother me as I watched her kiss her husband directly opposite me. We had spent the evening with the majority of the evening at the bar with the majority of the cast of 'Bite' who had arrived early.

As I showered, I caught a glimpse of my thigh in the mirror. It was covered in soap for a moment, and instinct made my hand touch the scar briefly. It felt sore and I wanted to scratch it. I found myself scratching it a little until it bled. The distraction made me stop staring at my own reflection and I allowed the warm water to wash it clean.

Soon afterwards I lay on my bed, glancing briefly at the last text from Sam, which was a basic 'I love you' message. I knew that I shouldn't respond just in case Luke observed it. I closed my eyes and soon I slept.

\*\*\*

# The Light Of Friendship

I dreamt of that evening one year ago. I could hear my argument with Jack and the subsequent fight. I watched as he raced into the shadows and I could see my bleeding love before me. I cradled her and I cried.

I was awoken by the urge to urinate and I glanced at the time on my mobile phone, it was almost 3.00 AM. It was freezing and I raced the bathroom. The sound echoed around the room and for a moment I wondered if I would disturb the neighbours. After I rinsed my hands in the sink I made my way back to the room. Something was wrong. I could make out a bulge in the bed where I had slept. It moved slightly.

"Who's there?" I questioned.

"You took your time" She purred.

"This isn't fair" I felt a tear form in my eye again as I inched closer toward Margot. She lifted up the blanket and invited me under, I nodded and obeyed her silent request, "I cannot believe a whole year has passed"

"Scrumpy" She comforted almost as if I had not spoken and she embraced me, wrapping her leg around my hip to bring me closer to her, "Please don't leave me again"

"I have to go" I whispered, I wanted to kiss her.

"It has been a very long year without you" She snuggled into me, "I have decided that I want to do something special for the anniversary"

"I was going to light a candle..." I began.

"A candle would be perfect" She sighed, "But I was thinking something more permanent"

"What do you mean?" I enquired.

She pulled away a little and looked me directly in the eyes, "We need to be together"

"Together" I repeated, almost chorus-like.

# D T Lewis-Dayle

"We can be united forever if you really want to" She kissed my nose and allowed her fingers to stroke my beard in that way that I liked, "There is a beautiful ravine nearby and if you were to jump we will be as one again"

She stopped talking and rested her head on my chest, and I adjusted myself to comfort her.

I drifted off a moment later.

The cacophony of birds awoke me as the sun rose a few hours later and I was once more alone. I dressed in jeans and a shirt and waistcoat before I ventured down to the restaurant for breakfast, leaving my mobile and wallet on the bedside table because I had no use for either at this moment in time. Margot played on my mind so I chose to sit alone away from my lover and her husband, and later I stepped into the grounds of the golf club taking advantage of the woodland and I followed a footpath for some time.

"There is a ravine nearby" Margot's voice repeated to me.

"No" I insisted, aware that although I was alone I may just bump into someone at any minute. With a panic I glanced the vacant area.

"We need to be together" I was almost certain that the wind was mocking her tone and I scanned the area. Nobody lingered in the vicinity and I felt a little comfort in that, she continued, "Join me, and prove that you love me"

I did not want to listen but she enticed me. She seemed to be luring me deeper into the forest, and I obeyed my mistress. I followed the soothing sound of her voice off the call.

"You don't love her" She taunted from an invisible force, "Come to me"

# The Light Of Friendship

An unseen hand guided me as she spoke and I urged myself not to see my Baby Doll but her power was greater than my will. A gust of wind would reveal her face behind a nearby bush or tree, or in the shift of the leaves above my head and at my feet.

"I miss you" I found myself muttering.

"We will be together in just a few minutes" She sighed.

After a few minutes walking, the breeze stopped and I paused at my location. The cold skies were beautiful and embraced me with a sense of calm.

"Jump" She whispered one last time.

I scanned the area and I could hear the rough sound of fast flowing water nearby, and as I glanced downwards I could see my siren bathing in the stream. She seemed to call for me.

"If you ever loved me" She taunted.

I closed my eyes and opened my arms. The wind felt so welcoming now and I felt as though I could fall forever just to be with her.

"Stop" A familiar voice called and I felt his hand touch my shoulder, pulling me back from the void.

"What are you doing?" I screamed, pushing Chris backwards.

"I sensed that you needed some help" He muttered, and I noticed that he was bleeding. I did not think that I hit him hard enough and I instantly felt sorry for him.

"It's my Baby Doll. I don't know how to explain it but..." I panicked, and I paused, "How did you know where to find me?"

"When I couldn't get through to you on the phone I asked around and someone said that they saw you walking this way" Chris explained.

I recalled that I had left my mobile in the hotel room.

"What are you doing here?" I repeated, I had no idea how he had gotten here so fast.

"I knew that you needed a friend" He spoke calmly.

# D T Lewis-Dayle

I turned to face the ravine again and she was no longer calling me, "She's gone"

"I think that it is time that I told you the truth" He sighed, but I concentrated on the waters below.

"Margot wants me to be with her. I think that I would have jumped for real" I changed the subject without knowing. Although I knew that she was not there I willed her to be in the fast flowing stream. I wanted her to lure me again to prove to my friend that I was not losing my mind, and I began to ramble.

Reality returned to me after what seemed like an eternity. Chris had taken a seat next to me on the edge of the ravine. The temperature had grown colder but I had not noticed until I saw my friend shiver. I took my waistcoat off and placed it caringly around his shoulders.

"I don't deserve a friend like you" I surmised, "You came all the way out here to find me teetering on the edge of a cliff about to jump for the ghost of a woman that died a year ago"

He remained silent, and I knew that was my cue to continue. I took a deep breathe.

"I miss her every day and I think I will for the rest of my life. I think that is why it could not work out with Wolf or Polly Anna" I smiled just thinking of the women that I attracted and then a flash of Sambuca crossed my mind, "I have a married woman back at the hotel who wants to run away with me because she doesn't love her husband"

"Sex is a way of moving on from the death of a loved one I suppose" Chris responded to my silence.

"I don't love her though" I confessed, "Last night I dreamt that Margot was back"

"Could it be just guilt that today is the anniversary of your engagement and if so would you wake up tomorrow feeling different?" He questioned.

## 19 – Whatever Happened To Taryn?

His words hit me hard. Today really was the anniversary of our engagement. She had been gone for 364 whole days and while it was true that I did think of her every day, there were days when I didn't. I hated myself for even letting myself forget her so easily. It reminded me that occasionally I could not remember her face unless I peeked at a picture of her on my phone.

"I think that it is time that I confessed to something" He broke the silence.

"What?" I replied.

"Remember how you looked after me when Taryn left?" He sighed.

"You miss her don't you?" I recalled that day in Middleton. He smiled and I knew what his answer was.

"She was the love of my life" He eventually confessed.

"Then I want you to go and find her" I wanted my friend to be genuinely happy, "When we get home I want you to pack up and go on the adventure of a lifetime to win her back"

He smiled and let out a chortle before he sighed, "I cannot"

"Why?" I questioned.

He did not raise his head as he continued "She was my perfect angel"

"Sounds like you have given up already" I responded.

He rose and brushed off some of the fallen leaves and dirt from his jeans, "You don't understand"

"What aren't you telling me?" He was beginning to annoy me now. Surely it was my turn to make my pal smile and if I could get him back with the woman of his dreams.

"Do you believe in angels?" He asked as he tossed a stone into the water below.

I laughed.

"Taryn was a guardian angel" He continued.

"Then how could she leave you the way that she did?" I asked.

"Tell me that you trust me Lee" He spoke calmly.

"Implicitly" I responded.

"Then it is time" He smiled.

It was then I noticed that he seemed to emit a white hue around his entire body. The temperature seemed to warm as the light around my friend seemed to intensify and I felt at ease.

As the brightness faded it did not bother me that we had relocated from the edge of the ravine to the cemetery. He seemed to guide me to the bench and I listened to his softened tones.

"Taryn was working the day that you saw her in Middleton" He began, "You may recall the white forensic tent nearby?"

"I thought something had happened to you" I confessed as I remembered how my heart sank and believed that she had hurt him.

"In our job we meet those that are about to pass over and make them comfortable for their onward journey" He continued.

"I don't understand" His words confused me.

"In the forensic tent was a young lady who had been killed in a car accident just hours before. It was an unplanned procedure so we were unable to ease the pain when it was needed" He explained, "Taryn had to work hard to calm the casualty. Her identity was compromised when you saw her and she was taken so that she could not be identified"

# The Light Of Friendship

"Taken?" His words were scaring me to a point that I believed I may have been drugged during breakfast which could explain how I had ended up here in a cemetery hundreds of miles away from where Sambuca was waiting for me.

"When an angel is identified the powers that be take them in what to you perceive as a violent storm. She was erased from this life and I will only see her again if my identity is noted or if I complete my twelve missions" He sustained, "You are mission number one"

"What the fuck are you on about?" I spat.

"Your death was pre-planned and I have been sent to guide you...." He started.

"I am not dead" I laughed his comment off.

"A little over five years ago, it was a normal autumn day and my day was full of the usual things that I would do that Friday. I finished work early and I had a few drinks with my friends and then I had a burger with my dad before I went to bed" He was telling me a story that I had heard before somewhere.

"You died in your sleep of an undiagnosed brain tumour" I concluded.

He nodded, "The priest in this church was my father"

"You're lying" I shook my head, "The vicar's son wasn't named Chris...."

"His name was James Birks" He interrupted, "I could not keep my real name when I came back...."

"Have you heard yourself?" I did not believe anything that he said. This idiot was talking about angels and the fact that his girlfriend was a celestial attendant of a man who sits on a cloud judging the human race.

Although he did not answer me, I followed his eye line to the gravestone that the priest once stood at, and it read 'James Lucas Birks, son'

"She was there for me when I passed over" He eventually muttered, "She helped me to adjust to the after-life. She was with me when I took the first soul"

"Wait..." Was he about to say that he was a grim reaper or something?

"My first charge was an elderly man named Charlie who played bowls and had a great circle of friends" He recalled, "I didn't think that he would ever accept that his life was over. It was beautiful when he did"

"What are you trying to tell me?" I forced the words out of my mouth.

He turned to me and placed his hand on my shoulder, "When did you last see Margot's grave?"

"I haven't been since the day we buried her" I confessed.

"And why is that?" He pressed.

I shrugged, "I think that I haven't accepted it..."

"May I take you there now?" He seemed to guide me and my feet started to walk in synchronization with him. I felt frightened, yet somehow comforted as we walked.

Her gravestone gleamed in the sunlight as we approached. I remembered that she was buried just out of the shade of a giant elm tree that she had once admired on one of walks. She had explained to me that she used to read her stories under a similar tree as a child and I thought that it was a perfect resting place for her.

"You have seen her a few times now haven't you?" He smiled.

I nodded, "It hurts me to know that for every breathe that I take, she doesn't"

"Tell me what happens when you see Baby Doll" He probed me to respond with a gentle raise of his eyebrows.

# The Light Of Friendship

"My heart beats so fast that I feel that it will burst out of my chest. When I am holding Margot I am complete" I felt a tear form in my eye.

"Do you feel anything else?" He seemed to bring me out of a trance.

"Yes" I recalled. I had never thought of it before but just before I saw her at any point over the past year my stab wound would cause me a little discomfort. Sometimes it itched or ached in a way that I had to touch the scar, "You know all about it don't you?"

He nodded without speaking.

"Why is that?" I questioned.

"Take a look at the grave stone" He gestured toward it.

I did not want to because I knew what it said. I had spent a long time wording the scripture that it was etched in my mind.

"Look at it" He urged, "When you see it you will know"

"It says her name" I began to stress.

"Does it?" He was now closer to the stone than before, and he began to kneel.

I joined him, and glanced at the name.

"Lee 'Scrumpy' Napier; Died a hero"

As I read my own name I froze in fear and then screamed.

D T Lewis-Dayle

## 20 – January

My mind was ripped in two. Just moments ago I was sitting on the edge of a cliff about to end my life and now my best friend, a mother-fucking angel, was telling me that I had been dead all along like a Spielberg movie or a Dickens character that was being shown his grave on Christmas Eve.

Everything seemed to slow down. The robin that was hovering nearby was moving lethargically away from us as I screamed and the people nearby did not react but I could see that they too were moving at a snail-pace.

I don't know how long I screamed or what happened immediately afterwards. I had walked away at some point and I rested on the steps of the church opposite James' gravestone. Chris had sat next to me holding my hand as I wept and I tried to take everything in.

"This past year has been like a dream" I concluded.

"The attack happened just moments ago. Time is moving at a different pace for you" Chris explained, "When you die you can go on and on until you are ready to take the next step"

"Is Margot ok?" I asked.

"She will be fine" He assured.

"And that is my body in that grave" It was a statement rather than a question.

"Of course we all have a decision to make when it comes to our time to move on" He added.

"Are you telling me I can stay here and be a ghost or something just to look after her?" I queried.

"Something like that" He allowed himself to laugh a little.

"There's something you haven't told me" I guessed.

He turned to face me again, "You do have a choice Lee"

# The Light Of Friendship

Fear tore through me as I took his hand, "What do you mean?"

We found ourselves back outside Woodies and it was night again. In the distance I could see the scuffle and I could hear Margot cry out. I could see myself and Jack in combat and as a knife glistened in the darkness I noticed that it was about to be buried into my thigh. We became static and Chris stepped in front of me.

"In about 3 seconds, that blade is going to going to pierce your femoral artery and although you will not feel it you will bleed out quickly" Chris explained.

I knew a little about human biology and although the vision ahead was on pause, I knew that on the night in question I recall being stabbed and had nursed the wound over the past year. I was also aware that in my reality Margot was dead and I was about to see her being stabbed in the heart like I remembered. I was thankful that I could not watch her die again because the pain the first time around was unbearable.

"This fight is happening right now" Chris continued, "Jack blamed you for him serving some time in prison when you robbed the bar"

"I know I understand" I nodded, "But please done make me watch her die"

"She doesn't die" He smiled, "In your mind you survived the stabbing and instead you mistakenly believed that Margot was the one that succumbed to Jack's rage. What really happened is that you die tonight on January 13th and not her"

"Then why bring me here?" I grabbed his lapel, I was angry and wanted someone to blame.

"You're a good man Lee Napier" He removed my grip from him and he turned back to the carnage before us, "Which is why you get to choose whether to live or die"

"I get a choice?" I asked.

# D T Lewis-Dayle

He nodded, "You can go back and live your life with Margot, or you can accept your fate and become an angel like myself"

"Become an angel" I repeated.

"You will be just like me…" He began.

"But Margot…." I interrupted.

"She will hurt for a while but she will move on" He seemed sincere, "She will always remember her 'Scrumpy' and there will be times that she will want to be with you. As an angel you can watch her from a distance to guide her on her way"

"But she cannot see me as Lee" I guessed.

He nodded, "Take a seat on the wall and think about what is next. When you make up your mind you can choose. There is no time limit"

"If I chose to live I will get the love of my life but then I lose my best friend" I surmised, "And if I choose you then I lose her"

"A friend can last a month or a lifetime, and it is why you called them a friend that matters" He advised, "Life isn't about the way you live it, it is about the cards we are dealt and the game that we play. I will be that one person that you met once on the set of a music video and the person that disappeared into the abyss. You'll probably remember me for a little while, and when the time is right but I will never have been"

I understood what he meant.

"I think you may have made up your mind already" He grinned.

"I don't want to go" I confessed, "I have never had someone like you before…."

He took my hand, "You've made the right decision"

He was gone before the words left his mouth.

"Chris" I whispered and allowed yet another tear to fall, "I don't know what to do…."

# The Light Of Friendship

I don't know how long I waited. The past twelve months skipped around my mind and as I glanced back over to the fight that was frozen in time, I knew where my heart belonged. I vowed to myself that I would always remember Chris, and I rose.

D T Lewis-Dayle

# The Light Of Friendship

## EPILOGUE

I awoke with a start. The bed next to me was empty and my heart pounded in my chest. I wanted to call her name but something inside me stopped me from doing so. I clambered out of the bed and raced over to the calendar on the wall. It was January 12th and circled inside the date was a note that Margot was out of town with her girlfriends.

I quickly dialed the a number and as soon as she answered I interrupted her, "I love you Margot Drake and I don't want to spend another minute away from you"

My next call was to Cassidy to tell her I was not coming in that day and she agreed to cancel the party that evening.

I put some food down for Macy who gave me a nonchalant purr before wolfing it down quickly, and I dressed in my best jeans and jacket and before long, I boarded the train and eagerly anticipated her face as I arrived. I knew that I had made the right decision.

I located them at the hotel as they were checking out.

"What's wrong?" Margot panicked as I raced towards her, "You sounded weird on the phone..."

I stopped her with a kiss and then I lowered down to my knee, "I was going to wait until the party tonight...."

"Lee stop" She urged, "I know what you're about to say...."

"I know and you were going to propose to me" I interrupted, "And I cannot wait to spend every waking minute kissing you, and making you the happiest woman on the planet"

"I love this" She smiled as she wrapped her arms around me, "What has bought this on?"

"A friend" I confessed.

As the words fell out of my mouth, I could not think of this name.

D T Lewis-Dayle

Printed in Great Britain
by Amazon

81369417R00071